*My entire life I knew, and many others knew, that our
daily bread was itself a kind of scripture of our origins, a
taste track of our lives. It is a lie that food is just fuel. It has
always had layers of meaning, and humans for the most
part despise meaningless food.*

– Michael Twitty, **The Cooking Gene**

To Jameson,
Eat good – in all
things.

ELIJAH DOURESSEAU

THE LONG TAKEOUT

SHORT STORIES FOR THE HUNGRY SOJOURNER

The Long Takeout: Short Stories for the Hungry Sojourner
© Elijah Douresseau

Print ISBN 978-1-66789-612-0
eBook ISBN 978-1-66789-613-7

YOUR ORDER IS ON ITS WAY

 THIS COLLECTION CAME TO ME at some intersection between music and trying to do a few other things of the soul. I had an idea of what I wanted to write next, but it wasn't working out.

The thing that was at the back of my mind was how much the feeling was almost identifiable by way of the proverbial sophomore slump. No one told me the sensation, the season of phenomenal complacency could occur after you moved mountains to get the second novel done.

What happened to the third time being the charm?

I was trying to activate something within the parameters of the expression. I felt even better about what was shaping up to be my journey. The problem was that I assumed too much before I started.

So I ventured down a path of wanting to write something different for book three. I simply needed to. I'm already considered a strange novelist, but by my own standards, I needed to work on a project that occupied a different form of playing with convention than the first two books. I ended up driving a stick shift, and I wasn't able to figure it out on the fly.

I then started to embrace a certain commonality I had known, for so long, but had escaped me. At one point after undergrad – and beyond my limited stint in grad school – I fooled myself into thinking it was beneath me. And then, in the quiet gestating of ideas, and believing there was some way to give them room to grow in a dirty light, I arrived at this short story collection.

It allowed me to do a few things I had been itching to do creatively, but gently – as to not scare off my reader – I got to do several things at the same time. While still keeping to the restraints of the medium of storytelling, the project ended up transforming. And tectonic shifts began to give way to new forms and structures for the manuscript.

Maybe this is my way of micromanaging how the short stories come across because I'm afraid you just won't get it.

Though in the course of considering whether or not to do the forward myself, something else emerged: this is another way for me to communicate the whole collection. It is the thank you card you get for that artisan book cozy you ordered on Etsy. The seller and artists are just grateful for your interest and your business. And since I'm not running a storefront, hawking my books (though the idea of a book bakery does intrigue me...BOOK PREMISE FOR #7!), I figured I'd do the courteous thing and send my gratitude ahead.

Read the book however you see fit.

It just dawned on me that people may not read a collection of short stories from top to bottom. It's the most acceptable non-linear reading, outside of magazines and newspapers, that won't burn you for skipping the narrative line. But you may want to start with the intro and finish with the outro. Any order in between is your conviction to do so.

The only other additional advice there is, is to consume this the way you would an album. To the above point, going in order provides an optimal reading experience, but I think I tried to be of the world a bit and composed a body of radio singles.

That's it. Stop listening to me in your head, and enjoy *The Long Takeout*.

TABLE OF STORIES

WHAT FOR? (PROLOGUE)

IT WAS A MOVE RESERVED for parents. For girlfriends. For artsy subscription services. But there it was, a care package on the living room coffee table.

It was not his birthday, not some other special occasion. He never told anyone he was homesick, mostly because he was stuck at home – and down in the dumps. It had been a hard year.

He was at work. His mother had brought the decently large box in.

After the layoff at the community social mining startup, he was only able to find something temporary. And part-time.

He never really cared to tell anyone.

His parent was not even sure. What he did between the hours of noon and six-thirty was strictly required for income. He rendered a service that resulted in money to do things. To maintain a constrained, basic standard of living. That was it.

The job was a start, but he could no longer afford his one-bedroom apartment.

The short-distanced memory he could not seem to get rid of was making that call to his mom. He had to be an adult and ask for help. To vaguely, but loudly enough, ask for his bedroom back. It was the resting place he forgot to swear to never return to. For an open-ended amount of time.

Surely - most assuredly - he would be out of there by the end of the year. In a good eight months.

He heard about so many of his friends' parents converting their old rooms into offices or den spaces. Thankfully, his mother was too old and nostalgic for such a thing.

The problem was that he also talked a good game. And when the mysterious box arrived, it was October.

He was too successful, for anyone who was within earshot of his voice. Restoring justice – this, and sixty thousand followers – that. So he moved away and moved in quietly. He could not face his friends much anymore. He had gotten busy all of a sudden. Always had another thing to do.

As soon as he was without, that was when the family functions started. October. The last fourth of the year. Normally, gatherings were opportunities for self-advertising the grownup twenty-six-year-old would have loved to have seized, only to tell anyone who would have listened how much he was crushing at life.

Cousins, aunts, uncles, new girlfriends – anyone who had forgotten or was not aware of what he was doing for a healthy living, and however else he was becoming a beacon of skillsets in his work and professional community – all at the gatherings would have heard about it.

Lately, he could not muster the energy to go, to keep up the same amount of enthusiasm as before. Back then, he knew he would have been able to leave those gatherings as an utterly independent adult citizen, with matters to see to the next day.

After life felt like it was socially over, there would have been no good reason for him and his mother to show up from separate vehicles since they were roommates. His insistence on the nature of their relationship. Not hers.

There was an elaborate guise he vowed to use if he absolutely had to see his extended family, the likes of he-said, she-said. It would have worked. Mostly because the kids at the mini-reunions, however young or grown, would hang with each other. And the parents, who were always the adults, would also tend to stick with each other for the evening. If anyone asked, he merely gave his mom a lift and was going to drop her off on the way home.

He was no fool. As many times as he decided not to go to the family events, he always requested his mom bring him back a plate. He was usually vain in those spaces, but his family was a people of good food. The leftovers would yield at least one and a half meals since his momma was heavy-handed with the portions. One less lunch or dinner he had to worry about providing or paying for himself.

His final resort to getting out of going to see his relatives was making it look like he was busy with something that could not wait. Chances were it was connected to work, as his lip service would put it, when his mother would inevitably ask why he could not join her. But she had to be okay with him not taking her. Or him not tagging along. One of several terms for staying home with his roommate parent.

Day in and day out, he was retreating into himself. Without knowing who he was. Without an interest-piquing highlight to mention.

It was rather interesting, he thought – in more than one instance, that he had gotten the most rest he had ever received in the last few years. Sleep. A gracious gift from the sandman he did not care much for a year ago.

It was a lonely life, featuring only him and his mother. He felt the pressure to keep a low profile from even those superficially closest to the inner sanctum of secrecy. Those next door. He tried to keep plausible pretenses up for the neighbors as well. People who knew he had left the nest ages ago. Until he accepted his current predicament.

He no longer felt it necessary to perpetually lie about or embellish who he was or what he was doing. In many cases, he could back up his salesman skills. But even carnival barkers and professional mourners needed to take a day off. And those employed souls were involved in way more colorful work than he could muster for the grueling season he was in.

Whatever minor triumph his dilapidated work ethic and ego managed to hold captive every so often, he did nothing to deserve the rather large parcel that was waiting to be opened.

He was in such a place in his life that he went to the bathroom for a spell, just to check his dusty Amazon account and make sure he did not accidentally leave any of his luxurious subscriptions active. Or that his account had not been hacked. Though he could not imagine, in any universe, why someone would want a piece of the sorry, soggy mess his life had turned out to be.

There were no alerts about his information being compromised. Then again, why would the package show up on *his* doorstep if his card numbers were stolen?

He ate his dinner with his mother, a weekly condition of residing in his childhood home – rent-free. His mom's insistence. Not his.

He did his minimal business to appear to be up to something productive since he did care a little bit about how his overall presence came across to anyone else. He did not bother to open the stacked piece of mail until late Friday night. Four days later.

The package was addressed to him. But his mother's home address was used. Someone knew of his whereabouts, besting his elaborate schemes to ensure he cut off any and every avenue to asking what he was up to.

No name from the sender. Just an address. One he did not recognize. But it was from the same state. There was no end to the possibilities as to who could have sent such a perplexing thing to him. A matter to preoccupy himself with over the boring hum of his current affairs.

When curiosity could sustain him no more, he grabbed the hook of an old wire hanger to break the seal to the box's packing tape. Beginning to unbox the contents, he removed some newspaper and packing peanuts to an interior of snacks – a treasure trove of gummies, chips, and other indulgent treats.

It took no time at all to recognize the common denominator for each item. They were the junk food selections he and his friends practically lived on in college.

Whoever packed the contents also included the nibbles he went with during various emotional shifts around midterms and finals. Savory into sweet. But never the other way around.

Precious time was spent on the wrappers. They were color-coded, a well-affixed sticky note on each branded bag.

And a letter. A secret admirer. A guardian angel who knew he was craving some late night processed salt – his soul food – but could not afford to splurge on any.

He wanted to explore the box further, but he could not bring himself to read the letter just yet. Seemed there was enough to examine and consider before getting to the reason for the spontaneous support.

But he could not investigate even the contents. He just had to sit, compelled by an unknown force to do so. He marveled at someone who did not care about any of his efforts to save some of his dignity. Just that they saw him, recognized him in an eerie way, and thought to send him some much needed care.

He busted open a bag of some of the gifted chips, to help him contemplate an inherently communal universe he was attempting to run far away from.

GRILLED MOON CHEESE

"WHAT DID YOU HAVE FOR dinner last night?"

"Did I hear that correctly? My last meal for dinner?"

"Ten four – or however you confirm the correct information. Uh, over."

"Let's see…I believe last night was fajitas. Though it was far from the tempting, sizzling kind you get served at an establishment. Not even a Del Taco for millions of miles."

"Chicken or beef?"

"Yes, for the chicken. With some not so sautéed peppers and onions. The side of rice was surprisingly good. And I had a brownie for dessert."

"I usually have some pretty decent leftovers when my dad orders the fajitas. I'm always doing some super quesadilla with too much filling."

"Leftovers are a great luxury, as we don't get any refrigeration in space. At least not for food anyway. Just enough room to store the dishes, heat them, and dispose of the containers."

"You get any hot sauce with your meal?"

"Now that would have been a decent ask. I'm the biggest fan of chili sauce on a lot of my food. Been up here so long, I can't remember what I would always use."

"Sriracha is my favorite."

"Sriracha! That's it."

"Hey, kiddo. Only a minute until class and you are not about to get this janitor in trouble with the high school brass. Finish up."

"Gotta go, Hank. Talk to you next rotation. Say hi to the stars for me. Seventy three."

"Counting on it, Cassandra. Godspeed through your studies. Seventy three, my friend."

Talking to an astronaut – one who was actually in space, was something Cassandra Shoume was all too certain she would never get tired of.

For the life of her, she knew it was a lost cause to make the first time they made contact unmemorable. An encounter she would take with her where ever she journeyed across the globe.

Cassandra did not even want to be an astronaut. She had her sights set on acting. She studied enough and fantasized a good amount to know the experiences she had with Hank for the last few weeks were the things of Oscar acceptance speeches, of magically portrayed roles that generations would watch over scores of lifetimes.

But all that ego stuff fell away, too. It was just the mere act of connecting with a disembodied voice, how simply incredible it was.

She was a faithful and believing churchgoer with her family on weekends. But talking to Hank seemed to open a window to other things that were possible in this life. Where the seen and unseen met for a reality that made her heart submissive to the mysteries of everyone's existence.

And it was all a complete accident.

She and her few school chums who befriended the eccentric janitor, Mr. Gus, with his conspiracy theories and giant heart, happened along when he could not help but flex his ham radio set-up in his working quarters.

It was an impressive sight. Something out of a movie with a big budget for elaborate, rundown-looking set pieces.

Mr. Gus was going to take down the establishment, one lunch break at a time. There was a whole network of ham radio enthusiasts doing whatever they wanted as amateur radio operators. The janitor had his sights set on fighting the good underground fight, but with a radio show named The Mister's Mid-Day Mouthful Munch, it seemed as if he was aiming to do a smooth jazz hour over the airwaves.

As cool as the equipment looked, ham radio operations were intricate for the very practical reason of receiving and sustaining clear signals so content could successfully be broadcasted to listeners from all over. Against any professional equipment or studio setting.

On the fateful day, Mr. Gus had a hard time broadcasting over his usual frequency. Nothing was working right. And in a fit of frustration, the dingy headphones he tossed at the contraption made the frequency dial skip to the International Space Station's signal.

Being classic Mr. Gus, he grilled Hank nice and hard about confirming who he said he was. Not much later, in a burst of excitement, he grabbed the closest students and pushed them into his glorified closet of an office. Cassandra and her two friends were mostly willing recruits.

When asked enough times about where he was exactly, the astronaut corrected everyone's assumptions, telling them he was likely above the school – just really, really high over it. The space station would eventually drift out of range, but on the course of service it was currently on, it would gradually drift back into signal.

Most times contacts were made, it was between Wednesday and Thursday, either by morning break, between morning classes, or by lunch.

There was way too much exhilaration in the first meeting. As soon as everyone understood the actuality of talking to a being, somewhere semi-unfathomable, in the greater universe, Cassandra, Mr. Gus – everyone had their own set of twenty questions.

No one realized how many inquiries they had saved for such a person as a spacefarer. But they were the things everyone thought about at night, before their eyelids held their minds prisoner for the deep ride into the black of an REM cycle. They were the what-ifs, the hope there could be something beyond the monotony of getting up to do one thing for half your day – that you likely did not want to do – seasoning in a few meals, only to return home to get ready to do the same thing the next day.

Mr. Gus had deep, soul-searching questions about extra-terrestrials only Hank could give him a satisfying answer to. Though the sanitation engineer always suspected off-microphone that the space-walker was hiding government secrets from his answers.

Brenda and Hank were fans of the same sports teams, except when it came to baseball, so the astronaut professional had a fun enough time catching up on the play-by-play action from the last bout between franchises. Especially from Brenda's super fan perspective.

Frankie, the person closest to wanting a career in anything remotely as near as being an astronaut, had questions about the complicated systems work Hank and his Russian partner had to do to keep the station humming along as the fine spaceship it was. Anything along the lines of the coding software that supported their operations analysis on the ground, Frankie was all asks and ears.

And when Hank finally convinced Mr. Gus – after interjecting on Frankie's turn, about whether or not his partner from Russia was a spy looking to do him in on some tangled espionage mission, Cassandra's mind went to the mundane. She had other TV and film observations, like everyone else, she wanted Hank to confirm; superficial things, like using the restroom in zero gravity, or if space shuttles were actually built for any kind of defensive maneuvers.

But she chose to stay on the topic of food. Also just as shallow, but Cassandra asked with keener interest. They were questions that largely occurred once everyone got serious about their cultural exchange campaigns.

That was the first time. Once it was clear doing press with an astronaut was always going to be a high-profile affair, due to the sheer volume of voiced wonders and inquiries, the three friends and the janitor decided on contact rotations.

Hank assured the quartet they were a fun bunch to make contact with, so he would also try to reach out, whenever he approximately was where he was hovering then.

What was the last thing Hank ate? That was the engaging question Cassandra decided to go with during the first radio meeting. It appeared there would be more opportunities to ask questions and just gush about how cool it was to talk to someone in relative outer space, but the food question kind of stuck.

Maybe it was still connected to some flight of fancy the fifteen-year-old always wondered when watching the latest sci-fi blockbuster, but the girl did want to be an actress.

At her age, tender but cooking, Cassandra knew she was interested in film. Being in them. She knew she was all too qualified to get an agent and get roles at her age. She had those things set up and was featured in her school's theatrical productions. But she felt like she was not getting something right about the craft.

It was a confrontation with the theoretical. It was the philosophical embrace of doing something as foolish as acting like you were doing something, along with others who were acting like they were doing other things – to collectively portray, however softly or intensely, a thought about their place in the world.

These were thoughts that were empirically true, through millions of trials of human data, without submitting anything to anyone for validation. But they were truths that were more visible through enacted statements that touched people. The practice of coordinated theatrics was the cultural force that inspired and challenged and opened windows to the beautiful absurdity of life.

That was acting to the high schooler. Not in so many words, if she were asked about what she liked and wanted to do after all her formal schooling had been completed.

The profession made people and companies lots of money, bolstering profiles, deserved or otherwise. The status of a successful acting career was a powerful, societal preference for the famous Cassandra did not take lightly, no matter where she would eventually find herself in the industry workforce.

So maybe her talks with Hank were an ongoing interview for research purposes.

When it came to acting, Cassandra was most fascinated by and most preoccupied with getting down the convincing look of food consumption portrayals.

Commercials had the signature fake bite of enthusiasm, to elevate the food product. Those actors had to make the food look enticing.

Sitcom characters played with the food on their plate. Enough to convince the viewer that in their television-verse, they ate food, but the act was ninety-nine percent staged. The constant turnaround and callback jokes in the dialogue were supposed to be the real sustenance.

In TV, there was a lot of resetting of scenes and shooting those scenes from different angles. So for the sake of continuity, the food had to stay intact in front of the actor.

Movies and hour-long TV dramas were in league with each other. Or they were the fringe outliers. The food in those productions was the most real. The actual eating came forth from the static of interior or exterior settings. The meals were consumed for dramatic effect, demonstrating heart and mood, and character, as much as the dialogue did.

Cassandra observed that the best actors did not look like they were eating food. They were. That was what the viewer saw. But the young exhibitionist witnessed hunger.

The food was a manifestation of that. It was the metaphor, the signifier through which desire and motivation could be communicated.

But true hunger, true desire could not be fulfilled. That particular longing was meant to breadcrumb the viewer's entertainment. Keep them watching. Never quite conquered or satisfied.

That was for life, out of the screen.

The girl understood enough about the nature of sets and the art form to know the on-screen narratives, fabricated by productions, were in heightened universes. They were special worlds where more things could happen or not happen, as a result of the characters' choices interacting with every aspect of their environments.

Part of the art meeting commerce, in getting studios and customers to sign on to the movie, was playing with that very assumption, of characters having dominion over their perceptions of their lives – their vague parallel universes that mirrored the viewer's.

Hunger was one of the great tools of filmic storytelling, to give a character their personality. Good or bad, hunger excited movement. It made things a little more interesting to witness on screen. And if there were any practicality to a scene or an exchange, be it set in a diner in the sparsely populated countryside, or a greasy spoon on a crowded New York street, food was the thing that told you what the character wanted. What she truly ached for.

The surface was food in those scenes. But it was usually a lot more than that. In a lovely kind of outer space of its own.

Cassandra managed to research the component of acting quite extensively. As it turned out, there was much to examine and study about eating on screen. Nothing quite concrete in books, but concerning everything from interviews, to the advent of spit-buckets and actors' riders; and the recent years-long Korean phenomenon of mukbang, the actor wanted to get good at eating.

Hank had an interesting look into needing to eat with a certain kind of motivation, the likes of which Cassandra never thought she would have access to. Needing to eat, just like everyone else, but needing to in a high-stakes manner that affected his survival. He needed to ingest food in such a way that he could finish whatever space mission he was on to get home safely. And since he was in such a privileged position to do it in a reality that most others would never experience, Hank became the perfect specimen for wrapping her mind around addressing hunger in a new context.

The girl was sure, space role or not, it would impact her inner textbook of eating on screen for the better.

So that was what it boiled down to. What did you have for dinner last night?

Hank was kind enough to play along. And it just became their ritual. Their code for allowing the conversation to go where ever it went after that.

There would never have been a time when talking to someone in space would not be inherently cool. But there was a make-believe quality to the conversations that constantly warmed the girl's heart. It felt like acting in a movie that would never be released. But for a time, the actors and crew were content to keep doing what they were hired to do on set.

"November, alpha, one, sierra, sierra," Cassandra called out.

It was her turn in the rotation to make contact with Hank. She managed to convince Mr. Gus to let her try during the nutrition break between second and third period. But she only had fifteen minutes.

"Wasp, mango, five, doggy, taco, foxtrot. Carson, California."

Cassandra put out her identification for the radio waves, to more crackling silence.

The fizzing over of static was a space vessel of its own accord. Mr. Gus was the only officially licensed ham operator out of the bunch. He had the most experience, but he also claimed he had never quite gotten used to whatever would be on the other side of the low or steady hissing of radio noise – to make contact with another life force. More of the excitement of the hobby to behold.

"Wasp, mango, five, doggy, taco, foxtrot station, this is the International Space Station. Good morning, California."

"Hank!"

"Cassandra. Hello there. Aren't you supposed to be in class?"

"It's all over! The zombies have overtaken us! You are our last hope."

"Funny. Gotta say, it was a lot funnier the last several contacts."

"I have to make sure the signal is clear."

"The cry for help from the mutant killer bees was my favorite."

"So, what did you have for dinner last night?"

Uncharacteristically, Cassandra asked the question to silence. Nothing for a few long seconds.

"November, alpha? Hank?"

"Still here, Cassandra. Was just grabbing my breakfast."

"Eggs? Pancakes? Sausage?"

"Sounds perfect. But not today. Fruit and toast this morning."

"How's the fruit prepared? You guys get slices and dips?"

"I'll have to remember caramel dip for next time. I'd probably dip more than my bananas or apples in it, too. But no. They come in their original forms, like on Earth. It's a mass of food so they're pretty okay to pack as is."

"Do they taste different up there?" Cassandra asked, in her question element.

"A little. Mostly because they're young fruits. Can't exactly afford to have ripe candy from nature here to risk rotting."

"Just put it in a loaf or something."

"It would be the saddest fruit loaf in the universe," Hank laughed. "I want to know what was on the menu last night for dinner theater."

Cassandra originally explained to Hank that for every show or movie that existed, there was likely a complementary food and beverage combination that could be paired with the content. Like a bizarre wine and cheese duo.

Hank did not watch much television on account of him being an astronaut. Though he did manage to consume a little Game of Thrones in space once, since that was the biggest on the planet, in its day.

"Superstore and Red Baron frozen pizza. Pepperoni. Classic crust."

"That's the Walmart show, right?"

"Loosely based on, yeah. It's a workplace comedy in a grocery store, so I always think it best to pop in some sort of TV dinner for the watch."

"You know you aren't in space, right?" Hank asked. "That's all we get up here. It has gotten better over the years. Actual chefs get to design the meal plans now. But once this is all done, years down the line, if I have space food at seventy-five, it'll be too soon."

"I gotta honor the theme. Art has to imitate life, and life has to imitate art. Cutthroat cycle."

"By my count, you only have a minute or two before you have to go imitate a good student."

"Dear Hank. I only slack off in second period because I've finished with my testing. The first student in class to do so, by the way," Cassandra responded.

"Don't let up. And on our next contact, you can help me make a birthday cake for Bogdan out of the sweets up here."

"Watcha got?"

"Mostly brownies, so it'll either be a chocolatey masterpiece, or a sweet mess."

"Sure," Cassandra chuckled. "Bell just rang. Seventy three, space dancer. Until our next contact."

"Seventy three, young lady. Excelsior, into your studies."

To Hank's joke, Cassandra did feel she was returning to the ultimate make-believe.

She supposed school for a teenager was not the most enjoyable third of a lot of students' days. She carried a healthy amount of cynicism for needing to go to class, at the same early time, all of her life.

She did well enough in her studies and was surrounded by an ample number of passionate teachers to make learning a great deal less of a chore. There was also a more than decent amount of performance to being a student in class that the artist in Cassandra could not pass up. Art imitating life.

But she was stuck in a hard place.

Hank probably had bad days as well. Even in space. Everyone did at work. What if he got sick or was not feeling good? He could not exactly call out and snuggle up at home in a half attempt at playing hooky – just to get a breather.

But at fifteen-and-a-half, Cassandra was feeling the itch to get into the universe that felt so big around her current job of being a student. There was so much to do and try out, including getting her acting underway.

In the same instance of her angst to grow up, she also could not have been more terrified of leaving her safe haven of school.

Did she have to have everything figured out by the time she would have graduated high school in two years? She knew that was not a requirement. But she did have vision of where she wanted to be. And how far away she was from getting to that height. There was just too much that could happen before then.

The universe of the Internet did not help. A deep black space of multiverses in its own right, the girl had Web MD'ed herself long before she realized she tunneled down a hole of terrifying outcomes and social media comparisons.

To the best that her experienced information, mentor wisdom, and overall worldview would allow, her aim was relatively simple. Cassandra wanted to be an actress, at the core of her aspirations. Her alimentary fascinations in front of the camera made up a particular track she wanted to be on. Friends would guess it was a quirky interest within wanting to professionally act, but eating food before a production crew and staff was the vocational task to obtain. Cassandra took nothing about acting more seriously.

She wanted to be known as the performer who ate in the most elevated way possible. She would get an award for doing it in the right film one day. At least a nomination.

College would be a larger part of her training. Her parents were not going to allow any other means of experience to exist without first starting with a post-secondary education. Undergrad was the bare minimum.

Her mom and dad were on board with her acting goals. The medical contract administrator and the mechanic business owner did not quite get it beyond a basic understanding of the art form, but they knew she had a passion for it and they had seen her flourish in plenty a performance space by fifteen years of age. So the support was there.

A small part of them hoped she would fall back on something else after getting her Bachelor of Fine Arts, accurately suspecting the life of an actor – short of mega success – could be a struggle for more than a handful of years.

Cassandra was okay with the prospect of slumming it to do what she loved. She was an artist romantically intertwined with the concept, to a decent extent, of being in that position.

What were her acting goals? They were not as fuzzy anymore. Emotionally, she saw something proprietary that could be her own. She was happy to do something on more of the traditional track with an agent, and with an undying penchant for soul-crushing rejection after auditions. The love for the form of acting and eating was on the screen. She would work to eventually get there.

Until then, experimental theater was the mission. The colleges and universities she had the most interest in had robust theater programs, and healthy film studies programs with plenty of students needing talent for films as school assignments. There were also conservatories attached to the most prestigious ones. She set her keener sights on the schools that were not afraid to leave everything to the students, including how the stage productions were to be experienced.

College would certainly have its merits. Cassandra knew she would have to keep her grades up to enjoy anything that was truly hers. It was at this crossroads that she got the idea.

Flash dances for the new age had recently re-emerged to become all the rage for the latest social media trending topic. Being of her particular artistic persuasion, she participated in many of them. TikTok made it too easy. But what about doing the same thing for eating?

The girl was lucky enough to see drive-by theater on a subway train when she visited an aunt and uncle in New Jersey last summer. It either came in the form of an acapella quartet or a three-piece music ensemble. Several dance crews were sashaying their way all over the tri-state transportation system. There was an improv group once. Cassandra had the most fun watching them.

Why could not the same thing be done with someone or a couple of people having a meal? A dramatic monologue or a well-staged argument? The social experiment of it all excited Cassandra to the point of trying something out at the Third Street Promenade. It was the officially unofficial alley of artsy panhandlers in Santa Monica.

She borrowed something from Death at a Funeral. She loved both the Chris Rock version, and the Matthew Macfayden British version, so she did the eulogy monologue from both films at two different restaurants.

She had a friend record from far away. To not upend the candid drama in people's faces.

Cassandra handled her acting business in the patio dining areas of the hot chicken place and the Johnny Rockets. But it was LA, in beach bum Dogtown. No matter how many swanky boutiques they filled the glorified strip mall with, witnessing someone talk about their dead parent very morosely and loudly was just not strange.

But it gave the girl courage to dream about a whole network of drive-by theaters. Something to astonish and delight as you were going about your errands. And it was all going to be endearing, through the vessel of consuming one's meal in a public place; an ultimate push from someone's environment to embrace the ordinary and the boring with all their might.

Since Cassandra was an actor by design, she had a knack for imposing drama on the smallest things. It was a peculiar bemoaning for life being cruel and unbearable, where others saw no such intense fires. But if she had a little more time to explain her case, there were just more trying days to see her dreams through than there were the smoother ones. Her constant was the inspiration to be the weird dramaturge in her adult life. On other days, she was terrified of needing to – having to – strike out on her own one day. Past the well-wishes and the, "You were so goods," she was going to be an artist in the sky, trying to work towards the planet of success with its rings of existential contentment.

Cassandra had had an especially rough week prior to her next attempt at making contact with Hank. She did not get the part of her choosing in her high school's spring production of Mamma Mia! And, cursed be her way of art, she was taking rejection a tad on the rough side.

She could not even play the race card. Another black girl was in the cast, co-starring as Sophie.

Cassandra was still in the musical. She had not much of a song and dance bone in her body, despite the flash dances. She was willing to learn, however begrudgingly, because of the bigger artistic obligation to the principle of there being no small parts. She just thought she would have played a killer Rosie - in the multitude of the character's non-singing scenes.

The girl could have really used some extra-terrestrial words by the time the cast list had been posted.

Thank goodness it was her turn in the rotation. She was actually the only one left of her quartet to attempt to make contact with Hank regularly. In the course of half a semester, it was too much of an effort for everyone else. Even for the engineer-in-training Frankie.

Mr. Gus would try to say hello once in a while. But mostly to back up his ham street credit of talking to a living, breathing astronaut. He got way more of a kick out of telling people he spoke to someone in space. "That way, I got 'em right where I want 'em. For other need to know secrets of our universe," he would put it.

"Hello? Hank? You there?"

Cassandra was halfway through her break period. She could not get a response to the space station's call sign. Only endless waves of crackles.

It was not a good day for her to miss out on something that, though it was always going to be plain breathtaking, she had gotten used to it on a human level. Like Hank was a friend at a local senior home.

She had tried all the other formal calls for contact, to no answer. She eventually resorted to using the receiver in front of her face like a cellphone – trying to get past a bad signal.

But nothing.

"Wasp, mango, fi—"

"Hank!"

"No. Sorry. Hank is busy on a job in the storage bay."

"Bogdan? That you?"

"Cosmonaut Bogdan Lebedev, at your—"

"Any idea if Hank will be done soon?"

"I'm not sure. We have not seen each other in a few hours. I am happy to speak."

"You know, class is starting super soon. I should be heading back."

"If this is Cassandra, Hank tells me you usually are trying to skip class, in some form or manner."

"That jerk said that," Cassandra smiled. "Tell him I'm going to class early to spite him."

"I will. Be well, little girl. Don't forget, cosmonauts get lonely, too."

"Yeah. My bad, Bogdan. Hope you enjoyed your birthday surprise."

"It was the most delicious mountain of sweets I have not consumed in a long time. Thank you for giving Hank some wisdom about it."

"Seventy three."

"Seventy three."

Static.

Cassandra could not believe she blew off contact with an astronaut, just because she was not talking to her favorite one. But there she was.

She needed to connect to a higher power. She guessed she confirmed she was willfully monotheistic in that sense. But it did not help to try something new in frequently occurring spurts of anxiety. She prayed the next time would be different, and Hank would be available. A lot of the way she navigated her day depended on it.

It did not take much longer before Cassandra and Hank were busy speaking to each other again. The actress, in her auteur neuroses, made some big deal about something she did not do, but thought she did. It frayed their relationship. Forever scarred. But Hank was just doing his job. She was trying not to make so much drama up with hers.

"I'm never sure what it means. If you're a Cal State mom, does that mean you're a mother and you attend one of the schools? Or are you the mother of a student who attends the school?" Cassandra wondered.

"I'm afraid I was never quite sure of that myself," Hank also pondered out loud.

"It's like – would your mom, if she got that bumper sticker, be a NASA mom?"

"That would be one way to tell the world you were a fake astronaut and a supportive mother."

"Does NASA even have a gift shop like that?" Cassandra asked.

"It's no gift store at Disneyland, but it's more than decent. Fairly elaborate, too. Hafta keep up with everyone else. Gets the brand out there, even more, I suppose."

"Happy you didn't ditch me this time," Cassandra mentioned, after a couple of seconds of mutual silence. She tried to keep some playfulness in her voice.

"Sorry, buddy. Duty called. Bogdan is a brilliant guy though. He was up to the task of filling in for me."

"I know."

"Says you kind of tried to squirm out of the contact. Which was probably a first for him on active work up here."

"He was great. For the few minutes we spoke to each other. I was… just being an entitled actress and having an off day. Didn't quite feel like talking to a stranger."

"We might still qualify as strangers, Earthling."

"But only a little," Cassandra replied, as a soft defense.

"I didn't know you were an actress. I was today years old when – I am using that phrasing correctly, aren't I?"

"You are. But you don't need to talk that way. Or feel free not to."

"Point is, that's your astronaut rock, isn't it?"

"That is better phrasing for it. And it never came up. I mean, I love it. Terrified of it. Not sure where it'll put me in the world. Seems hard to keep your chin up in an industry that is constantly telling you to do better because you aren't good enough."

Cassandra did not mean to be so upfront with Hank.

He asked.

She trusted him as much as she could confide in someone who did not seem to be there, in the flesh. She could say virtually anything, and knew Hank could not – or would not – care to tell anyone. No matter how lonely he was in a giant spaceship station. Nor how much Bogdan might have asked.

It was a funny image, the mental visual of Hank and his companion of the high heavens giggling like tween girls over a high schooler in distress. She doubted that was the cosmonaut's bend.

So she let it out, against her better judgement.

"Thanks for the candor. Seems like you'll be regretting telling me so much, but I must say…I'm grateful."

"Right. Hearing the waking terrors of a high school sophomore?"

"Experiencing humanity. We can't help but take it for granted down there. But up here, it's gold. I can read all the news I want in this station, but nothing will ever compare to talking to someone like you below."

It was the hyper age. The era of the voluminous inundation of whatever people wanted. Information was always first in that respect. Cassandra, her chums, and Mr. Gus were not the only people who were aware the astronauts were on an active mission in space. It was usually pretty close to front-page news. Cassandra could have looked up Hank and his entire history ages ago. But something made her resist.

She was not quite sure what it was. Or why.

Her generation helped spark the no-spoilers cliché, only to be the main perpetrators themselves. They needed to look up everything and left nothing to their imaginations.

Between Mr. Gus introducing her and her friends to the world and culture of hams, and talking to Hank for as long as she had, she realized she was exploring space herself. And for the first time, in a long time, she was mostly okay with not knowing what was going to happen next. It was the perfect refuge from what she anticipated and knew too well in the rest of her affairs.

"Flattered. But it's just me, Hank."

"Don't sell yourself short. I'm guessing your ambitions are better seen in the thing you love. Acting? Rather than school work?"

"You aren't wrong. But actors have to be smart and sophisticated, so the grades are up."

"The father in me shouts for joy. But you know what us astronauts are really good at?"

"Following directions? Moonwalking?"

Hank laughed like he had just heard the punchline to a top-five dad joke. "There is no better profession for following rules and procedures, but that is a small part of what we do."

"It is killing me softly."

"Indulge me. Because kids get this part. What did you want to be before aspiring to be an actress? Before you started to learn about the world and were taught to want to be one of only six or seven things? What was the thing you wanted to be before people said you couldn't be that thing?"

"Gosh…an Airbender?"

"The Last Avatar?" Hank asked, seeming pleased with himself that he understood a reference to something someone less than half his age mentioned.

"You are just about there. Yeah. I wanted to unlock the secrets of air-bending from unusual sources, like jet fuel and the gusts from birds' wings."

"Hmm. You were out there."

"Shut up," Cassandra laughed.

"I'm just saying, I'm in the confidence business. I'm the professional who says becoming an Airbender is possible."

"That seems…risky to tell a child."

"Not in the strictest sense," Hank replied, "but I'm an astronaut. Something people only really had a name for in the last hundred years. And even then, you think a lot of people know what this job requires?"

"Probably not."

"But that doesn't matter. The term for what I do came from fiction. From literature. And with the number of books and stories making a mega futuristic mountain out of my level of work, you'd think astronauts are as common as nurses or teachers.

"What are you saying, Hank?"

"It's possible. To brush your fingers against the stars. Just because people can't think of themselves as being something, doesn't change the reality that someone else can be that thing."

"Yeesh, Hank."

"I know. A lot of people can trivialize the Q and A we do with hundreds of classrooms all over the world. Including our front offices and Mission Control. But not us astronauts. Nothing will make us happier than raising generations of dreaming kids. Whether they enter our line of work or not. We want them to launch up to their own uncharted places and blaze a trail for someone else after them."

"We're all extraterrestrials. Waiting to tell someone we want to phone home."

"In a manner of speaking," Hank chuckled. "Is that the bell I just heard?"

"No…"

"Think it was. Now get out of here. Let your acting flood the world you navigate so that someone asks you how you do that."

"How *do* you do that, Hank?"

"Get on!"

The spacewalker was right. In the most 90's sitcom resolution way possible. But Cassandra knew one thing. She was done apologizing for the places she wanted to occupy. Done with apologizing to herself.

She was daring to hope again.

"Seventy three," Cassandra signed off.

"Seventy three and Geronimo," Hank signed back.

ALL IT TAKES

THEY SAT OUTSIDE. THE BEST excuse they came up with, that no one asked them for, was that it was a nice day. If someone did ask, the hypothetical answer would break down unmercifully, but they would have survived.

It was quiet. Almost in the way that things lost sound as they slowed down. Which was strange because they were on the sidelines of a well-trafficked neighborhood thoroughfare. But it just so happened to be the case that a certain preoccupation was at hand.

Everything was going as it usually did on the busy boulevard. And things usually went the manner they did, when there was a crisis having its way on the inside.

For Micha, it was the prime reason crimes occurred in the first place. The routine of life going uninterrupted for people and things. All they had to do was widen their eyes and look around.

And have a soul.

There were few other times he felt so out of place and yet felt so privileged to experience life in a way that he never would have – if something were not the matter with him.

"I'm going to need your head in this."

"Then why did you request a table outside? There are too many things happening out here."

"Got to kill your fish. Looked like you could use some air."

"Whatever the hell that means. I'm fine."

"You are a lot of things, Mike. But you are not fine."

"I just need some food."

"Relax. Focus on your breathing. We will get something to eat."

Micha's partner was terrifyingly calm under the circumstances of them needing to cool out at a restaurant table, in the near middle of the day. It was during working hours. A school day, by most assumptions. Cafes always seemed to drum up enough business on weekdays, somehow taking advantage of the late morning lulls when the majority of would-be customers were earning a living – or slacking off somewhere.

"Try not to be so squirrely when the waitress gets to our table," Theodore added. "Last thing we need are suspecting eyes and ears."

"I'm fine," Micha measured out. With an ounce of tenseness.

"Killing someone—"

"SHUT up!"

"What I'm saying is," Theodore calmly started, "we got to keep things dandy. The most important thing right now is just what's in front of you."

"The menu."

Theodore showed the faintest smile, like a parent who did not have the heart to tell his child he was terrible at making his bed, but the kid tried.

"Yes. We just need some food, remember?"

Micha knew he was right. But the last person he wanted to be with at that moment was the very person sitting across from him. After the early morning they had.

He could barely stand to be himself right after it happened. Theodore was a pain from the start. But he was a friend, and he was useful. He had a desired skillset. Knew the business of their operation.

Under normal conditions, it turned out Theodore did not know much of what he was talking about. The man was a vague kind of cultured.

A blowhard at being worldly. Whatever he did when Micha and Cole were not with him, Theodore could never tell them or anyone else what he was specifically up to.

He had an alarmingly frosty head right after it had been done; assured Micha he was fine. Nothing would get traced back to him or what they were trying to do.

"Sushi *and* boneless wings? Can you believe this place?" Theodore asked.

"I've been here before. They make a good peanut butter and jelly."

"I didn't know we can order from the kids' menu."

"It's not on the kids' menu. They do have their version. But the adult one has bacon. And you get the full slice of bread. With a hint of garlic butter."

"Just seems so far the other way. Guess they have to fill this photo album of a menu with something."

They were at the Cram Café. A hipster Denny's on the corner of Ventura and Van Nuys in the San Fernando Valley. Their whole thing was doing food right, and sourcing it well. The famous counterpart was Micha's observation. The other assertion stemmed from Cram's branding.

It was how Micha consumed food that was not his. If a restaurant lived up to its literature, the lore the man could gather from slogans and other ad campaigns, Micha tended to veer towards their food. It could even be an unpopular place, with a selection of eats that were less than okay. If they served what they said they served, in essence, it was a place he was comfortable patronizing.

He needed as much comfort as he could squeeze out that day.

Micha liked things easy. Anything less than sincere brought all the other mess that life was too happy, too ready to dole out.

"You ever been to the nurse's office?"

"Mike, I believe you. Adults can eat pee bee and jays. I haven't had one in at least twenty years, but—"

"No. I'm just asking. While you were in school. You ever have to be excused from class while school was still in session?"

"Yeah. Probably."

"I would get bloody noses once in a while," Micha started, reflectively. "And as I waited to be cleared to return to class, with a wad of medical cloth up my nostrils, I would get this feeling."

"All that blood loss made you light-headed or something."

"Naw. I was used to that. I meant a strangeness. Towards all the stuff going on around me. Like, how would I ever have known what the administrators did in the front office? Or what the principal did when she wasn't talking to us at an assembly, or telling us to quit running in the halls?"

"Sounds a wee bit too deep for a kid," Theodore returned. "I mostly remember being excused from class because I had just given the teacher some lame reason for ditching a while, after being allowed to go to the restroom."

"Didn't it make you feel funny? Seeing all the habits and practices of people when you weren't supposed to be around? And then you were, and it made you feel…omnipresent?"

"So you're God now? What in the hell are you talking about, Mike?"

"Never mind."

Micha was feeling that same sensation from all those years ago. It had eked up in other forms, at other times of his life as he grew older. But for an off-feeling that was impossibly hopeful, one he could not quite identify further, he was reminded of how it felt when he was a little boy in school. Sitting on a bench, outside of the nurse's office.

Back then, it gave him a certain calmness. Reassured him of how much he was connected to other human beings, to seeing life unfold, however mundane. It communicated to Micha, to even his younger self, that everyone was playing toward a bigger reality. Otherwise, how could life happen – whether or not Micha was aware of it happening – in the specific form he witnessed with his own eyes?

As a man, that same ability to peer at life terrified him.

Sitting at a table, on a Tuesday morning, in a makeshift patio area of a restaurant – life, in its utter fullness of wave after wave of going on and on – Micha could not handle being hyperaware of all of it.

"My name is Susy. I'll be serving you today. What can I get you two to drink, to start?"

"Hi, Susy! Think my guy here knows what he wants. Why don't you circle back to me after getting his order down?"

"What will you have then?"

Theodore gave Micha a look. He needed him to act right. To order and eat his food, and then they could process how to handle whatever came next. What they could make come next, if they got out ahead of the incident enough.

"Let me get the chicken sandwich. Leave the pickles. I'll do the slaw dressing on the side to replace the salad. And your curly fries to go with it. 7UP, please?"

"Excellent," Susy said, gathering the last of her notes on the order. "Looks like I'm back to you. What'll you have?"

Theodore smiled at his partner in crime. He seemed heartened that Micha was keeping it together. He proceeded.

"He made his sound so good, I'm in a hard place once again."

"Would you like to hear our specials?" Susy asked.

"That might be fun. Let's hear them."

Micha knew what was coming. Theodore enjoyed having fun with people.

A less discerning person would think Theodore merely liked talking to strangers. But that was only half true. He got people to talk so they did not notice they were running where there was no ground.

The thing about Wile E. Coyote running off a cliff, and realizing he was about to fall, was that he was being led to do so. Holding the speech sign up – right before the descent – confirmed as much.

The actions of someone else caused the movements of another to respond accordingly. But Wile E. would survive the fall, knowing full well that on the way down, he had been duped.

Victims of Theodore's stealth of tongue were not so lucky. He was gifted at gas-lighting the soul, only for you to have an off day and not know why.

"Today is a bit of a seafood surprise. We have tuna casserole potpie. Or a lox breakfast burrito you can try."

"What exactly is the surprise?" Theodore asked, adjusting his eyeglasses with scary interest – getting Susy into his realm of the waitress exposing herself.

"Sorry?"

"You told us what the specials were. Seems to be less of a mystery now."

"Oh. Yeah. I guess –," Susy began, trying to produce a professional response that would protect her gratuity, "management just kind of gave us a way to try to grab the customer's attention. There isn't much of a surprise, so much as there are two things available at a discounted price that involve fish."

"I see," Theodore trailed off. "Do you know what the revelation is though? The bit that isn't much to tell? I'd feel way more comfortable getting my food from someone who could unlock the mystery of daily specials to a paying customer."

Susy was at a loss for providing any more help. She was certainly more present. More immersed in the humdrum minutiae of the mental capacity it took to order something from a restaurant. Theodore had her wrested, full attention. And he likely wished, from where Micha was sitting, that she was a little scared – but largely felt she had an interesting exchange with someone who made the highlight reel of Susy's response to a loved one's ask of, "How was your day?"

"You've got me. Turns out 'casserole' and 'potpie' in one name are redundant. But it is decent eating."

She looked as if she were praying within herself that that little bit extra would have sufficed, and Theodore would leave her alone enough to get on with the only reason she was talking to unfamiliar people. Because she got paid to do so.

"Hmm." Theodore looked over his menu for a small moment more. Glowing in the commandment of keeping everyone suspended with what he would do next.

"Thanks for clarifying, Susy. I will have the strawberry and Nutella crepe. And I will wash that down with some chili cheese fries, and an iced tea."

The waitress made to grab the two menus. She was successful in taking Micha's. But Theodore had to keep his just out of reach when she made an attempt. Just to get one more victory.

"And that will be unsweetened."

"Sure thing," Susy weakly returned.

"Also, mind bringing out the fries when I'm about done with the crepe? Not much for drops in temperature when the food's been left out."

"Totally. I'll uh, have your dishes out shortly."

The waitress quietly collected the menus and made for the kitchen.

"You were brutal."

"I didn't know what I wanted. But she helped me."

"Thought we were trying to keep things simple."

"We're trying to keep things at a cool setting. Simplicity is more of a byproduct."

"Well, we need to think of something. It has to be thought out. It has to be airtight."

"We will get there. We've done enough for now."

Micha knew exactly what Theodore was referring to.

They were thorough. Left nothing up to chance. The damning trail might expose a couple of truths, but not what exactly happened, or the body they made scarce.

Micha's thought process during their nearly occurring meal was very precise. They both got away with or were getting away with murder. Over brunch.

At the present moment, attempting to commit insurance fraud did not feel like such a punishable felony.

"So what happens after we get some food? It's kind of hard to think about three hours from now."

"You're fine company, Mike. But I assumed we would go our separate ways. I got things to do. And the day is still young."

"Shouldn't those other things wait?"

"As providence will have it, we're off the hook. Cole and I checked out the perimeter a week ago. No security camera close enough that would tie us to crime one or crime two."

"Which is crime two?"

"If you're asking about the second crime, I think you know what the first is."

"We eat and then just go on with our lives?"

"No. I'll be sure to call you on your birthday next week," Theodore added, with a fake gentleness."

"That can't be all we do. Getting away with this is one thing. But shouldn't we do something for him? Something we can—"

"Hold it."

Susy was returning with their dishes.

"Here we are," placing the food in front of its respective owner. "And let me know when you are ready for your chili fries. The chili sauce is being kept warm back there, so they'll whip up a batch of fries in no time.

"Chili cheese. Right, Susy? That's what I ordered.

More eyewear adjustment.

Everyone let the sting of the entitled ask hang in the air for a second longer than necessary.

"Oh, of course. A slip of the tongue. I'll check on you two in a bit." She hurried off.

"You really aren't bothered by this," Micha realized a little more fully.

He received the food. The smell brought him some comfort from the looming senses of character doom.

The dish looked fine. But he could not bring himself to eat.

There was no nausea. He was not sick to his stomach at the thought of ingesting something for a meager appetite. His human function to consume food just seemed to be turned off.

"We all hung out, but Cole was your childhood friend. Not mine."

"So I'm the only one culpable in all of this?"

"I'm not going to ask you again. Eat your food and simmer down!"

There still were not a lot of people in the restaurant and outside on the patio. There were certainly enough patrons and staff present to know that someone just raised their voice at another person, at their social bubble of a table. Grounds for instant attention. And people being on edge about anything escalating.

Never mind that the perpetrators also happened to be two black men. The only two black men in a Valley restaurant, for what was okay to consider as being the case for a while.

Micha had no idea what Theodore was looking to do with the outburst. For all time, they were going to be the two African American males who had a screaming match at Cram Café. The profile could tie them to what happened earlier.

Enough of the stunt worked, in so far as the frantic one was embarrassed into being quiet for a spell.

Neck, hot. Hair, standing on end. Ears, also hot, Micha had nothing better to do than to fume at the man sitting across from him and force his food down. He had to learn how to eat again. Had to learn how to consciously taste what he was eating so the base form of his mind, which had not been sustained since around six o'clock the night before, craved more drop-off visits from his hands.

Theodore was never mad or frustrated. He got what he wanted. Some peace and zero talking.

The two ate in a stuffy silence. A couple on a bad date.

Micha focused on his food. Busying himself with finding the inconsistencies of the flavor and varying textures of his fries.

Theodore ate and incessantly looked into the dining room. Which is something he did on a typical outing for food. He loved to people-watch and eat like he was watching TV.

The skittish one was getting his bearings back. The hangry-ness to neurosis transition was numbed to the fulfilling power of salt, sugar, and drink.

"Gentlemen. How is everything?"

"Marvelous, Susy. Thank you."

Theodore was back to his chipper, suave self.

"How's my other order?"

"Sauce is still in good shape. Are you ready? Looks like you're just about done with your crepe."

"Almost done, but I'm not finished. Got to savor these last few bites. I'll let you know when I'm ready."

"No problem. I, um, shall return."

"Appreciate you, Susy. Bye-bye now."

She flashed an awkward receipt of such a farewell and walked off.

More hushed minutes ensued.

Then Theodore could not stop enjoying the last of his thin pancake in an audible fashion. The groans increased. The mouth sounds and gasps of pleasure followed.

"Hope you are enjoying that sandwich as much as I enjoyed this."

"It's working. I needed it."

"Lovely. Because the next twenty-four hours are going to be hard on you, Mike. You need to spend as much time not thinking about it as you can."

"You're sure we're in the clear?"

"You can never truly be. Professionals who are squeaky clean have gotten caught up, too. But it'll be years before anyone can even discover the body. By then, we'll be far away. In some form or way."

"How could the damn fool not get insurance after getting zoned for the deed?"

"That was always Cole, wasn't it?"

Micha could not help but laugh at the conclusion.

"We never learned our lesson. He always got the logistical things to do."

"And he usually came back with a righteous mess," Theodore added.

"But he was a good friend."

It was going to be the closest thing to a funeral the third was going to get.

It was pitiful. Reminiscing over a mid-day meal. Only the last two people to see and feel Cole alive.

Though it was efficient. The incident. The effect. The need for a repast.

"Mike. Buddy. You have to pull it together. You can't be crying in a place like this."

"Am I?" Micha quickly wiped away the streaks from his eyes. "Just um, in my head about him is all."

"I know. Crimes of passion get you like that. The momentary insanity. Doesn't mean he was not your friend. That you didn't care."

"I just hate not doing something for him now. And all the other stuff is flooding back. I needed that insurance money."

"Better drowning on the outside with bills, than being locked up and drowned with hard demons."

Micha was not so sure about that. Not anymore.

The feeling of vindication wore off too quickly. He had instantly played out a couple of scenarios in his mind. The first was that prison was coming and it was something that had to be done after committing murder. As natural as aging up into the next grade in school, bookended by graduation ceremonies.

You never think of getting away with it so soon. At least, that was not Micha's role.

He was only the initiator, the facilitator who put people and remaining resources in motion to take care of a bad breakup. He got just about everything in the splitting of shared possessions, and he had to pay for it. Houses were not cheap. Taxes on homes were not inexpensive. And the man still had to think of every other facet of living a basic life that required money.

The second scenario was how much of a prison you imposed on your life immediately following your participation in a major crime. Even amidst the debt, there was a small amount of innocence to getting after the means of living like most other people.

But after early that morning, Micha realized it was all playtime. He could not have real relationships with other human beings anymore. He could not try to start to cultivate a new bond with a woman – to eventually emerge with kids and college plans and pensions.

Life was a performance from the dumping of Cole's body, forward.

The fatigue, the anguish of getting out of bed, day after day, to look for a job would never bother Micha again. It was far from the worst feeling.

The attempt to live something of a normal life after that day would have to be a worthy distraction. It felt like one of the few things left to do that would not require remembering who he was, or what he was capable of doing to try to make life easier.

"You have to consider this day a brand new one."

Theodore had a newfound attentiveness toward his table companion. This time, the eyeglasses were adjusted tenderly.

"What?" Micha had sought shelter inside himself for a moment. He had not heard anything but his heartbeat for the last few minutes.

"Nothing should be hard anymore."

"I was just thinking that. I've been feeling it for the last several hours. But 'easier said than done' has never been truer. I'm pretty sure living with this guilt will be something that messes with me for the rest of my life."

"That is a blessing in disguise, my friend."

"I don't want it. But it's mine."

"You're understanding, Mike."

"I'm not so sure I ever will."

"You are not a killer."

"I can't be delusional about this, Theodore."

"You have this cross to bear. But it can't be for naught. Or else Cole died in vain."

"But he did. We had no business doing what we did. Before…"

"Certainly. Though I'm not so sure you would have this mindset if we were all alive and successful at what we tried to do."

"I just thought we could scam some money. In my wildest dreams, I did not see anyone getting hurt, or it going this far."

"And yet, you pulled the trigger. So what will you do about that?" Theodore asked.

"Don't add anything to it. Even figuratively. It's already bad enough what happened. Weapons were never involved."

"You're not hearing me, Mike."

"How's everything, fellas? Can I get you two more to drink?"

"I'll take more 7UP, thanks."

"And you? Can I bring out your chili cheese fries?"

Theodore turned to Susy and actively considered the question as he stared.

"I'll take the next course to go if it's not any trouble."

"No trouble at all!" Susy seemed relieved that was the extent of it, answering a hair too quickly after Theodore expressed his wishes.

"Be back." She walked off once more.

"How many times have you done this?"

"Not many. I'm in a mood so I figured the fries will sit well later."

"No. Cole. Or been an accessory to a…Cole."

Micha knew Theodore had seen his fair share of the bad stuff that happened in the darkness. It was one of the reasons he was recruited. He was their crime tour guide.

Micha and Cole were acquainted with the man from mutual friends. They hung out at enough barbecues and bar runs after work to develop a casual relationship. Knowing Theodore hustled in less of a legal way came in instances. A hook-up here and a favor there.

"That would not put your mind at ease."

Susy returned with Micha's refill.

"Here you go."

"Thanks."

"Can I bring you two the check, or are you ready for additional plates?"

"Could we enjoy more of the ambiance of the restaurant? Even if you were starting to close us out?"

Theodore's question posed yet another way in which someone could be menacing. He could not leave the poor employee alone.

"Oh, sure. No one's really here. Take as long as you need. I'll bring the fri— chili cheese fries with the bill."

"That would be excellent, Susy."

"You want to make sure she never forgets you."

"No, Mike. I'm here. This is what I'm doing. I owe it to her and my food and everyone else here to be present."

"How does it become more than a breathing exercise? When I'm home? Away from everything?"

Theodore took the question and held it for some time. He even took off his glasses, only to put them back on.

In the rarest of occurrences, he genuinely appeared to be measuring some consideration for whatever he was about to say. An ounce of sensitivity Micha assumed he only reserved for his mother.

"I'll say it again. Cole could not have died for nothing. The facts are, what we did back there was messy. And it was terrible. But something so awful has great potential in slapping you awake."

"I'm feeling it already."

"The sudden conviction to get your shit together?"

Micha nodded. Theodore had been in this space before. The hours after.

The first-timer had taken for granted how much the veteran, in whatever capacity, could empathize – or set the record straight.

Micha felt like he was back at the nurse's office. Emotionally, his young being would always rush to the phenomenon of being a fly on the wall to processes and procedures beyond his understanding. It was always just fun to watch.

The very first time he had to get his nose cleaned up at the nurse's office, it scared him how much blood could fall from such a small space. It got everywhere. The rivulets mostly missed his white uniform Polo. They caught his navy pants some. But his fresh, black and white Nike Air Structure Triaxes had been in a fight. Speckled with a generous amount of blood droplets, the nurse was beside herself, trying to figure out how to make the stains disappear.

Young Micha insisted the blood stayed on his shoes – to satisfy whatever complex order of street credit for third graders, who were sent away from the classroom, afforded him. Everyone could only conclude, upon his return, that something serious had happened and he needed attention.

That would further conclude that the boy had won at something. Socially bested it. But no one could definitively say what.

At Cram Café, Micha's perspective was shifted. The nurse was tending to his wounds and he was listening intently on how to prevent the blood from continuing to stream out of his nose.

Perhaps it came with being an adult. The medical stuff he tuned out and only absorbed as a kid – staunching a bloody nose numerous times – became the matter that defined everything else. The words. The length of time for applying stopping pressure. The lack of concern about a giant cloth booger stuck up his nose. Adult Micha simply had to get well.

"Here you are. Thanks for eating with us today!"

"I'm going to pay for our meals with cash and tip you with cash, Susy. No need to return until we are gone."

"Uh, yeah. You got it. Thanks. And take care."

Additionally, the last thing Micha wanted was to look the part. He could not run far enough from the drops of guilty blood. They were a shower, too heavy an effect from a cause Micha had too much of a part in. He imposed a reckless will on a desperate resolve to change his circumstances. He should have allowed some of it to be out of his control.

At least bloody sniffers in '91 were involuntary.

"With every cell of remorse in your body, in your bones, you have got to follow the meals."

"I do that enough on my phone."

"You don't. Nope. I'm not talking about Instagram," Theodore shot back. "The food you put in your body has an enormous responsibility now. Whatever you do that you can't possibly focus on because your mind and heart are concerned with matters of existence and eternity, work at snapping out of it when you eat."

"So the last hour was just some training thing?"

"We did need food."

"But Theodore. What do I do?"

The question got to the soul of the silent crisis. Getting away with murder. Micha felt the metaphysical stuff. But the how-to could not stop being a terror. Perhaps it would never stop being that way.

"You have got to feed yourself. Even if everything you put in your mouth has lost its vigor. Eat to get to the next stop. Things will fall into place."

"Alright."

"All right?" Theodore asked, getting to the soul of the crisis himself.

"Okay. I'll do it. I'll try."

"Good. Then you go your way for a while. I will go mine."

"The two stood up. Theodore sipped one more intake of his drink. He palmed the bag of chili cheese fries, like a football, and handed it to Micha.

"You changed your mind?"

"It is yours, Mr. Micha."

"I don't want this."

"Planned it all along," Theodore grinned.

"Seems like you're full, and you don't care to take home your extra baggage."

"You're refusing my gift?"

"I just had fries," Micha pleaded.

"They're the easiest thing in the world to eat. I'm quite confident you can go again."

"Real funny to gift me a variation of my side. THIS will be my turning point. For sure."

Micha was still on edge. They were biding time in a bubble of brunch and once it popped, the world felt cold and too infinite again.

"Ignoring your sad sarcasm. You are going to find that sooner or later, this manner of doing things will cross your mind. The relative ease of it taking care of immediate issues."

Micha had not even considered such a thing. To be a twice murderer, or further. How could Theodore suggest something so twisted?

But the morning had happened. And the man knew his partner was right. Unspeakable things could reoccur, even if Micha could disassociate from them in the peculiar way humans did.

"What time is it now?" Theodore asked.

"Quarter to one."

"Keep it. Don't refrigerate it. Eat it promptly at five. And put your mind to it. For the twenty or so minutes you eat it, fixate on the taste and the chewing. And get to the end of the container."

That was how it was going to be. A graduation under an overcast sky had commenced. Micha was no longer at a medical office in school. There was too much innocence to that.

He was receiving a prescription at a pharmacy. An oftentimes mundane errand to run, but something he just had to do for the rest of his life. Among other things.

"Can I at least give it some heat when I eat it?"

"From a microwave?"

"Seems appropriate."

"Those things will kill you."

Micha gave Theodore a look.

"Sorry."

"You have been just…perfect with words today."

"But wait – you, yourself, are not a killer, right?"

"I'm not."

"Then 'appropriate' need not operate hifalutin machinery. Take it with some liquor. That should be heat enough."

Micha kept the bag. He turned to go. A heavy-handed pat on his back signaled to him that Theodore was close behind. From the shade of the patio roof tarp, they stepped into the sunny unknown.

Micha turned around to his partner in crime. As soon as he was facing Theodore's direction, the man had already started walking off, leaving Micah a lonely patron at the café entrance.

He brought the bag of loaded fries to eye level. The small grease stains that formed all over the bag, which added shape around the fry container, reminded Micha of a coffin. He was not sure whose. But somebody he had known was resting inside the bag.

Maybe he did not hydrate enough during the meal.

He took the bag like Theodore handled it originally, but thought it better to support the chili cheese fries from the bottom. Hot, but safe to touch.

Micha moved his legs and feet down the street in the opposite direction, trying to visualize an appetite for five o'clock.

CAMP MUDDLED BROWN

AS A NINE-YEAR-OLD, BRANDON ADAMS could count on a few fingers the times in his short life he was deathly afraid of something. Most of the frightful subjects were inspired by movies. Films he was probably too young to watch, but he had a big brother. Only once or twice did these cinematic experiences inspire such a psychological manifestation of terror to take hold of not only his thoughts, but his body also.

He saw Children of the Corn one night. It seemed to physically grip his entire being, causing him to tremble under his covers hours after the movie had stopped and the lights had come on.

It was somewhat clear his inner-city reality with his mom and brother was far from what spooked him so, but it was that from which he could not look away.

The fear usually wore off. Took a week or two. He had to ruffle through the clothes in his closet. And check around the furniture in his room that would face him during the cover of the deep, late night. But it became increasingly easier to fall asleep, despite the monsters he knew existed – in some sense.

Months after this, Brandon found himself in an impossible situation. Because it was one of the most thrilling times of his young life, but he thought it a bit unfair to have to trounce so many lingering creepy things along the way. Creepy things that grew into worrisome things, that would lead to death.

The situation was at summer camp. Troy Camp. 2001. He and scores of fourth and fifth-graders, from different schools around south Los Angeles, were living the life of chaperoned independence on the woodland surface of Idyllwild-Pine Cove – due way east in the Golden State.

The boy took everything seriously about his major trip. The adult big kids, the college student counselors from the University of Southern California, told him to do as much – as a sacred privilege. But the call to be far away from Hoover Street, away from the strife of 'hood life and gang activity, was a compelling one.

At no other time in Brandon's nine years of living did the boy have the physical space and the vast periods – within a week – to see himself as an individual. To examine his habits and various behaviors as a living, breathing body with a mind and a heart, in a variety of situations. Especially as it related to forging friendships, and getting acquainted with a special girl.

The little boy, representing his elementary school with three other students whom he did not know, was utterly aware of himself for the week away from home.

What was more, Brandon had a feeling begin to grow inside of him at the start of the first night of his prolonged camping excursion. From the moment he woke up on the day he left, there was never a more exciting combination of nerves and anticipation to see himself apart from his mother, his brother, his classmates, or anyone else he had a relationship with.

As a pleasant interruption to see himself as a part of a greater world of systems, structures, and ideas, the counselors served Subway before the party took off for camp.

The departure site was an elementary magnet school that had an affiliation with the University. Brandon was told smart kids attended 32nd Street Elementary School, kids who eventually would be capable of getting into USC.

It seemed fitting that the academic setting would be the very place from which the boy's life would change forever. And what better way to continue to reinforce the tremendous milestone than with more food than the boy ever fathomed could be kept in one place for a group of people?

Brandon had never known a restaurant, outside of a pizza place, to prepare such a massive order of food for takeout. Scores of white, nondescript boxes held treasures of complete meals, comprising of an entrée, a side, and a dessert.

Normally, at the Subway restaurant, Brandon's mother would order his sandwich. On his own, he would request a bunch of stuff be put on his sub that he did not actually like. And he was not going to waste his mother's money, as she would have it. So she would get six inches of something advertised. Without chips. Without a cookie or a drink, because they had all those things at home, his mom would reason.

It was usually the Cold Cut Combo. It tasted enough like a sandwich, but against Brandon's young sense of taste, the main course either contained too much meat and not enough of anything else, or the other dressings made the edible submarine too off-tasting. The mustard, combined with the onions and another sauce the boy could not call by name, gave the food a sour finish to every bite.

But at the start of camp, before they even got to their great outdoors destination, Brandon was having a sandwich the way he thought it should have been ordered. The way he wanted it. As the Subway commercials confidently purported at the time.

There was a Cold Cut line. A turkey line. Ham and roast beef lines. The gems Brandon never got to touch were at his fingertips before liftoff to his camp adventure.

He hopped in the turkey line, happy to have anything but the ham, salami, and bologna coalition, and was soon opening his very own box to do with it whatever he wanted to.

He could have tossed the whole thing away if he cared to, he realized. Though he was way too much a fan of eating to commit the heinous but permitted atrocity of plum throwing away his meal, without so much as a nibble.

The box was its own Happy Meal. A sandwich, chips, a cookie, and condiment packets. Having their independence in full swing, the kids did not hesitate to cultivate their own bartering system of whatever they desired from other kids' meals. Cheetos for Doritos. A chocolate fudge cookie for a chocolate chip one. It was all safe to do because the kids had more than enough agency to do so.

Brandon even saw one kid with a box full of cookies. He was a good deal unsure of how the kid pulled it off, seeing as there were more cookies than the original components in his box.

The almost-camper got the sandwich of his choosing, but the cookies and chips left two things to be desired: Rold Gold Pretzels and an oatmeal raisin cookie. He did not even know Subway sold pretzels as a side choice. But the boy did not trade what was given to him after he had elected to receive it. In most cases, it probably would have been difficult to trade what he knew was the least favored chip and cookie combination in the history of chips and cookies. Even Fritos, while still at the bottom of the preference list, got way more play.

The boy found a group of boys to eat lunch with. They got on as friends, like they had known each other since kindergarten. He was careful not to be messy with his mayonnaise and mustard in the manner one of his new chums was dealing with his sub, getting mustard in the corners of his mouth as he took hungered chomps from his Cold Cut. That was not acceptable. Girls were present. And Brandon was fairly convinced, from too many sources to keep track of – if you asked him – that they were always watching.

The children soon organized into groups, filled the buses, and were off to an unknown part of their California home.

The feeling then was infantile. Not uncomfortable. Filling, mostly. Likely on account of the generous Subway. It gave Brandon the stuff of wanting to keep his engine going for something greater.

The only time the feeling gave him a bit of a twang in his belly was when the bus had to stop once they were winding along the steep mountain roads. Two kids had to get off to vomit.

"Motion sickness," he heard one of the counselors say. The boy had never been in a situation to experience or observe the health phenomenon. But it was terminology that gave his feeling the tiniest bite, and the new association gave Brandon the knowledge he had to go to the restroom. Nothing immediate. Not an emergency, as he had been conditioned to report by the teachers he was in the care of seventy-five percent of the time.

It was business on the back end of things. But he could certainly wait. Plenty of time for the familiar sensation to develop into something more substantial. He could hold it, as was the common jargon used to express the feeling – at the time.

He had bigger things to focus on. Sweeping landscapes. Mountains that he was closest to than ever before. And oceans for skies.

Brandon and the other kids soon arrived at the campsite, to a parade of counselors with nicknames like Salsa and Rusty McGee. He had to arrive on the grounds to realize they were not going to lodge in tents, but permanent, erected structures that served the same purpose.

The boy knew of cabins. The kid from the city had just never been so close to one, let alone interacted with one for outdoor purposes.

A tent dwelling seemed to signify a prime camping expedition, for however long, more than a cabin did. Though Brandon was grateful. He might have been lacking experience in the way of outdoor living spaces, but he figured a tent would have been an awfully cold stay. There were profuse warnings to pack sufficiently warm clothes, a sweater, and a jacket. Even in the summertime.

He was sorted into a cabin with nine other boys and two camp counselors. There was Mickey. He liked to speak as Mickey Mouse, among other voices of animated characters he thought endeared himself to the kids. And a more stern, tall college student with a lot of facial hair. He went by Dodger. And it was not because he liked baseball, to half of the boys' disappointment.

There was time to settle with your family for the week, as the head counselor on the bus put it, choose your bed and refresh yourself for some rally to attend before going to the mess for dinner – the first time Brandon would ever hear familiar words used for similar outcomes, in new situations.

But he prided himself on being a quick study. Being smart. It was why he was allowed to go on this trip and represent his school. The first in his family to go camping the way he was.

Though he would never admit his call of duty to anyone his age. Since it would have made him sound like he was a cast member of Barney and Friends.

The most fascinating of the two new concepts was the mess hall. It was another way of saying the dining room. Where, in the most predicted of outcomes, messes occurred from eating food in the space. Of course, the little boy, who would always assume he was ready for the experiences of a thirteen-year-old, thought the word was too presumptuous about the lack of care he would take to neatly finish the food off of his plate.

But Brandon could not help but think there was more to the term. Something he was happy to explore during the week, instead of asking Dodger, who first referred to it as such.

Getting to camp was also a rebirth, in a sense. The boy was determined to commit to memory all the information and preparation literature his mom was given to get ready for camp.

Everything was easy enough to understand. He also accompanied his mother on shopping trips to get the appropriate wardrobe for the week.

One thing that was stressed, and it was another relatively new concept to hold close on his quest into independence, was dehydration.

An unpleasant episode of momentary sickness that resulted from not drinking enough water. That was the long and short of it. And being as high from the familiar LA surface streets as he was going to be, interacting with elevation in a new way the boy did not realize was possible, water was going to be his best tool for navigating the foreign land he was in. It was his wand since he was an impressionable kid just getting into Harry Potter.

The water would also help him adjust to a higher altitude which would impede his ability to breathe at a normal rate. And he did feel it whenever he walked around the grounds. There was a slight fatigue he felt even walking the shortest distances.

If you asked him, Brandon would have claimed not to have any memory of his early months and years of life, of trying and trying to walk. But for a short time at camp – a day or two – the young boy felt like he was learning how to get his legs under him again. Elevations and altitudes made the camp its own dimension.

It also made the boy's feeling more of a deeply tuned sensation. Though he did not have to go yet. Peeing seemed to relieve his bowels enough.

The cabin of Wolverines, ten boys who thought it cool to be the same mutant superhero, as they insisted – over the animal – made their way up the hill to the mess hall. It was another decent hike for Brandon, acclimating to the essence of his surroundings, but he and the others made it.

The cabin groups lined up, single file, in front of what looked like the biggest building in the forested neighborhood.

It was a gargantuan cabin with a trim of bricks and stones. The wood seemed a bit more polished than those of the cabins the kids and counselors came from. It was half shelter, having a wide opening that large, wooden dining tables lined out from. There looked to be couches and a bookshelf full of board games inside, in one corner as well. So the mess hall was a place for a few purposes, Brandon quickly understood. Like a living room for a bunch of people.

The tables were the most eye-catching of the scene. They were dressed with utensils, plates, and silverware. Each had large containers covering the length of the tables, holding parts of dinner. The true identities of which were a mystery, at least for then, since the steam bubbles clouded the contents below the glass.

The most attractive element was the tablecloth below the table elements. A plaid, crosshatching of red Brandon had seen at plenty of other restaurants. He would not have acknowledged such things in the spaces he would have assumed the coverings would be present in. But he was in a new world with glorious accommodations. And to eat out at a restaurant every night with a group of friends seemed to be more than the right fit for his new and temporary lifestyle.

The other aspect of showing up for dinner that struck Brandon just as hard was all the girl cabin units that walked up from the opposite side of the hill. The camp was split by gender. Boy cabins came from the left. Most of the girl cabins, from the right. He felt like he was the only one to observe the other sex being present. Many beautiful young ladies he had not seen on the ride to the mountains from the school.

One girl in particular, seeming to be nearly as tall as her counselor, filed into line a few yards away. She had a head of short braids and barrettes that swayed with every movement of her body, like she had a mobile for a head. She had wide eyes, pools of movement and life. Her lips were full. She wore overalls with hiking boots and Brandon was enchanted. She looked like a sixth or a seventh-grader, and the boy had trouble looking away.

The intermittent gazing was enough for his stomach to remind him it felt a certain way about its present predicament. The soft feeling came back with a little bit of a nudge. Though nothing worth sounding any alarms for.

Once all the cabins were present, led by their counselors like some assembly or fire drill on the blacktop of a school playground, the announcement for dinner came. But first, everyone was going to partake in a few activities, to get the blood flowing and the appetites going – the head counselor commanded.

Brandon thought this was largely unnecessary. There was good-looking food wasting away from inactivity because the adults thought the kids needed to exercise first. It felt a little like preschool. Needing to song-and-dance their way through every activity.

The procedure for that dinner, and every meal after that, as it turned out, was to earn your place at your cabin table with your roll call routine. The Shibuya Roll Call. The head counselor and supporting staff would start with a little introductory tune, which would then call up the cabins to respond with their version of introducing themselves to the rest of the camp. Brandon had seen versions of it in live concert videos. He also did it at church. The person onstage said something that would cause the people in the crowd to shout something back, like some bizarre movie script.

The best boy cabin and best girl cabin, with the most well-performed routine – some sort of catchy chant – would get the privilege of being seated first and setting up their table for the meal. So they would have been eating sooner. The remaining cabins duked it out in who's-the-loudest competitions to get granted approach to their food.

The roll call talent show would have been fine to participate in if Brandon had not seen the most beautiful girl in the world at camp – the love of his life. The adults were asking him to act like a fool in front of esteemed company.

Though, because of his overcompensation to attempt to remain nonchalant, he was the most charismatic of his cabin during show time. And for that, with the number of laughs they received, they were granted first entry on the first night.

There were a couple of house rules to discuss when the Wolverines were seated. No matter what they were, Brandon made sure he was sitting next to the widest food container on the table. It also happened to be next to Dodger, but there were worse things to worry about.

The advantage to getting seated first, other than the spatial upper hand of being nearest to your meal, was that you quickly got through the two-drink minimum before getting started. Given their location, every camper had to drink at least two cups of water before digging into their food.

There were also table monitors assigned for each meal, to tidy up the serving dishes, plates, and utensils to be cleaned by the cooking staff afterward. Once the housekeeping was done, they could have at the grub, even if they were the only cabin to do so.

Dinner was served family-style. A new thing for Brandon. Outside of the weekends, and only if his mother was off or they were dining out somewhere, dinner was usually just him and his big brother. They definitely did not do the sitcom family thing. The manner of dining room eating that mostly existed in the distinguished TV universe.

On weekends, his mom would make the food. They were allowed to have their plates anywhere in the house, whether in front of the living room TV or their bedroom. With a tray, because his mother did not play about food stains on anything but dinnerware. A disparate experience, in any instance of anywhere but the kitchen table.

At camp – burgers, salad, and fries that night – they had to be efficient and orderly about sharing their food. Could you pass this, and can I have some of that? It was a pleasing machine, an aspect of Brandon's new residency that he was going to adore for the duration of his stay.

He heard an adult say once that you could not choose your family. The boy always seemed to be conscientious of that, but it felt more true being heard aloud. It also appeared to be the case for his cabin. He was assigned to be in a perpetual brotherhood with nine other boys that felt somewhere between familial and school-familial – his classroom.

Dinner the first night seemed to solidify the truth further because family mainly seemed to be who you shared a meal with.

There was another glorious thing: you kill it, you fill it. Not only was the format of their meals going to be a soft buffet one, but the system also dictated that if you grabbed the last portion of any of the meals' components, you had to refill them at the kitchen's service window. Assuming you and the rest of the cabin had not had your fills. Everyone had their weight to pull, and everyone had a responsibility to make sure the cabin was represented with a heart of service and diligence toward the present task.

And the food. Brandon was in no better a place to take care of his newfound self-ness than eating the way he liked to, with any amount he wanted on his plate.

The next thing to try to get right was getting up to get more food when the girl of interest was on duty to do the same thing. The boy did not know how often he would be able to interact with her, but being only feet from her was the next best thing. He assumed, without any prior information, she smelled like cherry ice cream.

The first dinner was mostly eating and business. More house rules from the counselors. Plans for that night and the following morning. They were going to clean up after the meal, return to their cabin to dress for the cold of the evening, and head back out for the campfire.

Brandon was feeling good in those moments. Eating. Carrying himself as a nation among many in the wilderness.

In seemingly disconnected moments, he did think about how far he was from home. And what his big brother and mother might have been up to then, content to relish the space between worlds that sat before them. The boy was going to be sleeping somewhere else from his family for the first time in his life. He had vacationed with his loved ones before and had slept away from home. But never by himself. Never to the tune of his own business with other people.

He could rationalize sleepovers existing in the real world, but where he lived, it was another fruit of taking up space in the television universe. In a few hours, he was going to do it for real.

The Wolverines headed back to their cozy cabin number six after feasting like princes. The evening sun had given the landscape a molten glow. Like everyone had heat rocks on their faces and in their chests. But it was also dark on the outer edges of the once inviting and lush trees.

Brandon was still mostly swept off his feet by the views, but he had seen enough horror movies that he should not have seen to know you did not go running into those dark areas on your own. Unless you cared for unwanted company.

Dodger was in their wooden abode first. There was a light in the cabin, though it was not the freshest bulb. But it did illuminate the space enough to alert the counselor to an eight-legged visitor on or near the mattress, against the right wall of the dwelling. And Dodger went low. So that meant the spider was around Brandon's sleeping bag.

"Fast little guy," Dodger debriefed the boys, "but it's gone."

What was not gone – in fact, what had come to infest Brandon's mind and extremities, was the horror film that had spiders front and center: Arachnophobia.

Unfortunate victims in a small town who fell prey to bites from exotic spiders. The arachnids hid in places no one cared to look in, only to place their foot in a shoe or take a shower with a web spinner that was happy to pounce in for the kill.

Brandon watched the film with his brother a few weeks before taking off for camp. His mother was away working so it was the perfect night to view the wonders of scare filmmaking.

Back then, Brandon thought he could outsmart the spiders. If he could catch them in the act of sitting in their webs before they caught him when it was too late, he could somehow keep the scuttling abominations at bay.

For a week, it became a ritual to check under and around home objects the boy never realized had a body or an underside for examining.

He did not see it in the movie, he thanked God, but the place Brandon feared a spider encounter the most was on the back side of his toilet bowl. The nether region he could not have cared less about before the film, but there he was, kneeling and sticking his head behind the toilet before he had to poop.

Being on the toilet was a time that, even at nine years of age, was sacred to the boy. Along with the release came a breather, a way to examine life and his present day from a different perspective. And really, he could just think about things. The biggest thought occupying his cells was the feeling of his presence from the gaseous smells of the contents of the bowl. He knew he was alive and making his mark in the world.

The sheer possibility of a furry, crawly thing threatened that serene peace. He was going to be damned if he would let a spider kill him in a compromising position. Creeping up his you-know-what. Or biting him on the delicate you-know-which.

"And this week, guys, while you're staying here, keep the hygiene going for us and yourselves, please. Shower. Brush your teeth. Use the restroom when you need to. Don't go getting all constipated on us. You will not enjoy yourselves being plugged up. Neither will we."

Dodger's speech came at the worst time. Until then, the boy knew the concept, knew the word, but he had not affixed a name to what was starting to tug at his lower half. But it was exactly what he was going to do. He could not get away with checking public toilets for spiders.

Until camp, Brandon was mostly content not to get bitten on the toilet at home, for a reason he could not identify – other than seeing too many similar situations play out on the small screen. He knew that was not how he wanted to end up.

Being reminded of the movie, he had already resolved to be thorough about checking for arachnids just about every time he was alone. And if he could not do that at camp, then he was not going to park his behind where he could not keep an eye on it the entire time. Or when he could at least be assured it was doing its expelling thing in a spider-free zone.

Peeing was always going to be permissible, no matter what. By the boy's logic, he could see his equipment when number one was at play. And he reasoned, if there was a sighting while the stream was aflow, he could always drown the sucker with his yellow-ish water gun. Or run.

There was always a certain amount of truth-seeking Brandon did with scary movies. The classic bit of rationality was, like with Children of the Corn, he was far away from whatever place the movie was set in. Also, the movie was not a documentary. He understood the formats of different TV and movie programs to know the tales of terror he and his brother watched were scripted projects on artificial sets, and featured a lot of special makeup.

The spiders from Arachnophobia were not from America. He forgot from where, but they stowed away in the country and started making lots of babies. Though the movie did take place in a small Californian town. The likes of which resembled the hills and outdoors of Brandon's present setting.

Even if Brandon did not find an exotic spider in the San Jacinto mountain-scape, the boy had watched enough National Geographic. Non-city spiders, the big, hairy ones with bulbous bodies and multiple, visible eyes, ate bigger prey. The daddy long legs he would find in his Los Angeles home could only dream of being able to take down the same kind of food. The follicle-laden ones resided in the very place where the camp was located.

So Brandon had successfully rationalized, and then unfurled his reasoning, to be certain that spider monsters lurked just beyond what was easily visible around him. And that one lucky, tarantula-looking thing would succeed in getting him good on the toilet at camp.

Just then, Brandon's intestines started to speak. They were a tad impatient. It was long past when he would usually have his stinky quiet time. And they were starting to complain. But the boy could keep it down some more. It was onward to the rest of camp.

The boy was able to sleep enough. He hoped he did a subtle enough job of checking his mattress and sleeping bag for creepy crawlies. He even did a quick flash of his portable light to make sure there was no funny business from a night companion he would have least liked to host.

The sleeping bag was the perfect scenario for a spider to catch someone unawares. He wondered why his current scene did not make it into the movie, but he was not going to let any multi-eyed thing rehearse its killer part with him. He could not even joke with the other boys, to soften his nerves, seeing as Dodger was a bit stern about the lights being out, and the noise being non-existent by a certain time. Mickey had camp preparations to make with some other counselors for the next day.

The thought, or series of thoughts that made Brandon go to sleep, was the other time zone his family seemed to be in. It was cool enough to be far from them in the daytime, sizable lengths away from the authority of their conservative views and their no's – whenever the boy wanted to do something they did not approve. But he was also away from them at night.

It was something the young adventurer certainly saw coming. He was going to sleep-away camp. That meant he was going to rest in a place he did not know, at least the first night. But there was a certain anticipation Brandon had for being around his family when it was late. The mandate on completing homework. The night shenanigans with his brother. The snack or two he would steal from the pantry right before his mom would ask him if he brushed his teeth for bed.

And the sleeping. If Brandon was not around to see it, to wish his family a good night – because he wished them a good night every night – did they actually sleep? Or could they slumber properly?

Of course they could. For something he was so excited to be away from, the routine of something familiar – for the thrill of something different – Brandon could not stop thinking about his brother's and mother's heads hitting their pillows. For the next handful of dark hours.

Did he miss his family already?

No!

But the boy wondered about this and pondered about that, concerning the goings on back home. Eventually, he forgot about spiders, and his brother's tightey-whiteys he was embarrassed to tell anyone he slept in, until he was fast asleep himself.

Brandon soon opened his eyes. It felt like a couple of moments. Morning had crept up on him when he rested his inset binoculars for any kind of frightening advances.

The cabin did not seem so strange in the early hours of daylight.

It was colder. There was a gray paleness to the interior of the cabin that had no real artificial light, or any other modern infrastructure in place, from what the boy could tell.

Sunlight awaited everyone outside. Its form glowed and cracked through most of the rickety surfaces of the cabin. The structure had more than a few of them.

The boy woke up feeling full. Not a sensation he was accustomed to. More accurately, his bowel clock was ticking. He felt a bulge in his midsection. However modest, it was starting to make itself known for every waking moment he did something, or thought about anything else other than sitting on a toilet in the restroom.

It was still manageable. He learned, while getting ready for bed the night before, that relieving himself on the frontal side of things, or farting

– which the juvenile, nine and ten-year-old boys in the Wolverine cabin quickly had grown accustomed to for sport, did help relieve increasing pressure for a time.

Everyone was dressed and soon headed out for breakfast. As far as Brandon was concerned, he was passing most of his test of being his own young man, away from his family. An eighty-nine percent graded paper he would have been proud to receive a B-plus on.

He did think about what his brother and mother were up to, when he knew what they would most likely be doing, but he still very much wanted to explore life on his own.

For a boy his age, coming from the neighborhood he did, college was the ultimate goal. Everyone around him, and the encouraging things he saw, made it seem more important than what he wanted to do after college.

Brandon was fine enough with his academic occupation. He still had to work hard. But the labors of his studying and retention, and his natural love of reading, were paying dividends when report cards were mailed home. And when the contents of his toy chest needed some sprucing up.

But the boy was most intrigued about needing to go to a far-off land in order to become an ultimate student, to take charge of a career. By his age, there was no not going to college. It had already been instilled by his mother and inspiring sitcom episodes. But what of the lifestyle of such a vocation? Of being a professional student within the living halls of prime academia?

Camp felt like practice for college. The two seemed to be comparable worlds from the boy's point of view.

Brandon, in his vast, but limited imagination – by way of experience and context – got to thinking about the prospect of going to sleepaway camp when the opportunity first presented itself during class one morning.

The outdoor adventure the week proposed seemed fun enough on its own. Like an extended birthday for groups of kids who only wanted to have fun. Great! He was on board enough for that. But the camp would be run by college students. Adult men and women living the life the boy was supposed to get to. So he also planned to conduct some personal research for the week, aside from experiencing the best kid vacation he could think of and take part in.

He had been around college students before, but never on his own. Never with miles of time and space to get information on what would be in store for him, in what seemed like an eternity from then.

Brandon liked his various thought processes when he was apart from his family. They were not too different from when they were together. But he could explore why he felt certain ways, could delve into what things were – in essence – and have time to acclimate the extended universe to his worldview.

He also wanted to show how responsible he was with being given the chance to be a little adult. Flossing, and changing his underwear when he was supposed to. Taking a proper shower.

Everything besides sitting on a toilet. For a mostly irrational reason. One he could never tell anyone else, but that was the line he had drawn.

The cabin made its way up the hill for the mess hall rally before breakfast. Brandon's girl of interest was looking rested and flowery as ever.

Everyone sang a couple of songs, and then came time for the judgment of which cabins would get to their seats and their food first.

The boy could smell the morning nourishment. Naturally, he had a bit of a sixth sense for picking up on his favorite meal of the day – even from the bottom of the walk-up.

He could smell the eggs and potatoes. See the toast and cereal. There was an unidentifiable protein maintaining its warmth in the same holding dishes from last evening. Sausage or bacon, no doubt. Brandon felt empowered to wish for both since it was a possibility, and none of his family was around to accuse him of eating too much.

The Wolverines were third to get seated that morning. Still the cream of the crop. But enough to grow a little ill at ease. The early victory made Brandon realize he would have to be a mature young man. He would have to soothe himself from getting too antsy if, competing for quicker access to future meals, his cohort would be one of the remaining eight cabins – with sleepy or hungry onlookers.

It was sausage!

The boys discussed their plans for the day. Hiking, crafts, trail maintenance, sports, and games. Not quite in that order, but it was a full day ahead. Brandon even got to ask both his counselors about college and what they did daily when school was their home.

Dodger was a Political Science major. In his third year. Mickey studied Computer Science. Graduating next May. He also got to ask them about their collegiate food options, which largely seemed like eating at a mall's food court every day. It was a distant dream of Brandon's that seemed as if it would come true eventually.

Everything he wanted always felt like it had to be an extension of getting good grades. But for endless options of customization and self-service, Brandon would oblige – like abstaining from opening gifts before Christmas day.

Breakfast came to a close. Brandon was on tidying duty that morning with Xavier. Brandon was meticulous, making sure his mom would have been proud of something he was not responsible for doing in his home just yet.

Though she would have something to say about his stubbornness with the nearest toilet. She would not be sympathetic to his concerns of cinema coming to life in the most deeply real ways. His present bowel state, worsened because he had two full plates of breakfast, was trying to make room for itself in Brandon's digestive system.

It had just dawned on him – a horrid realization – that the more food he ate, the more urgent a need he would develop for sitting atop a toilet. A sensation that would never have been a problem anywhere else but where scary movies seemed to be filmed - the camp - surrounded by forest.

But worse than a freakishly clawed man visiting him in his dreams, more sadistic than killer children, or homicidal clowns, was not being able to eat all the food he wanted. Even if there were no qualms with anyone over how much food he could stuff in his face, he could not, because of his increasingly full guts.

To make matters worse, Brandon got a taste of a specific tale to associate with his loving campgrounds. There was no more a need to imagine it. According to Mickey, it happened in the very place the commune stood.

Of course, it was years before. Years before anyone had the slightest spot in their eye to build a summer camp for little kids from the ghetto.

The Wolverines decided to take a night hike after their second evening singing songs and playing games around a campfire with the rest of the cabins.

It was early enough before everyone had to be inside their wooded abodes, so the majority of the mutant campers were too happy to check out the grounds under twilight.

Brandon wished he could have been more enthusiastic, but after lunch and dinner, and trying s'mores for the first time, his stomach was the furthest from being a happy camper. Some thing – many things wanted to come out, but all bets were off at night. So it resulted in a good deal of sharp discomfort. It was a constant punch to the abdomen that the boy could only absorb and place even lower than where his waste-producing organs were.

On top of that, once the Wolverines hiked a half mile behind the cabin, there was a clearing that overlooked a flat land of blackness. It was there where the boys gathered around Mickey, as he told them a tale of a family of four in an old town, whose father fell ill. They made some terrible decisions, forged agreements with demonic entities for the sake of the dying daddy, and then there was a great fire. They were not much liked in the neighborhood they resided in, the future site of the camp, so the authorities suspected arson with murderous intent.

It did not slow the family down one bit. They resolved to be together forever, and it was exactly what they did. The first firefighter on the scene discovered a charred, huddled mass and soon heard voices. The parents and their kids had stuck together through the best and very worst of times. Even in death.

It was a riveting narrative. Exciting. Scary; contained a Disney-esque theme of family values.

The ghost story was a thrilling thing to hear while in the company of others, with everyone's flashlights turned off. Though it did no favors for the growing gastronomic tension in Brandon's body. Any anxiety, or trouble he would feel mentally or emotionally, not to mention physically – it all amounted to more duress with which to get the food goblin out of him.

In the height of the quiet, after Mickey finished the story, Jose's back sputtered out in a string of farts. Everyone laughed, even Dodger, and there was a momentary respite from the chaos of life and the horror that could emerge from it.

* * *

THE REST OF CAMP WAS an amazing blur. There was more liberating food to be had, and more opportunities to fraternize with Melody, Brandon's crush. More instances of the boy striking out as a kid on his own.

But the need to poop. It became the camper's dark conscience. His quiet spice that whispered when they were alone together and howled whenever Brandon was in the middle of an activity with others.

He even considered giving the undying urge a name, but could not ultimately give his close enemy the dignity of a moniker.

The first-time wilderness lodger, on day four of his outing extravaganza, decided he had had enough gross pain in his belly for a lifetime. It was starting to affect his mood, the amount of food he cared to eat, and the way he could go about the still new world. Mostly because the stomach cramps made it hard to walk and not assume a position to empty himself on the spot. At no other time in the boy's life could he remember experiencing the pressure to get it all out, no matter where he was. He imagined he had more control over his stomach as a newborn.

In a moment of divine permission, there was some downtime between lunch and the Wolverines' pool slot. It was their turn to start the afternoon in the wet space, and they had to take their time to get ready and chill before heading over. So their food could settle, as Dodger emphasized.

Brandon started his break at the restroom as early as he could. They had about thirty minutes. And in nine to fifteen, he would be on the other side of relief. Ghosts and spiders be damned to hell.

But he could not do it. For the life of him, he could not make. It was the strangest sensation. He pushed and pushed with all the might his belly, hips and behind could muster, but he was not making progress. And the attempts were starting to hurt.

Then he remembered what Dodger said. Waiting as long as he had, had terrible consequences. The counselor, in his worst nightmare, could not imagine someone trying to poop after four days.

Brandon was constipated. Stuck in limbo. Ready to give the contents of his backside the swimming experience of their lives, but he was unable.

Then he thought about his family. How they would react if they somehow became aware of his current predicament. How his big brother would laugh himself to sickness. And how his mother might smile and make to chuckle, but would not go any further to spare the boy's feelings.

In that rock bottom space, homesick and on the toilet, Brandon felt the slightest movement.

Mickey peeked into the restroom and announced a ten-minute warning to no one in particular, but to everyone who was still caught between rest and getting ready for the next thing.

It was then that Brandon acknowledged himself. Not quite as a new person. But as a boy who came from a world all his own, into a new one. He was prepared to marry the two in a way that would shine only triumphantly in the boy's heart. It would inform other adventures of seeing and living that were sure to come.

So he pushed again. And there was a little more movement.

METER NOT APPLY

"DID I WAKE YOU?"

"No, got up a couple minutes ago. Was just brushing my teeth and freshening up for the day."

"That's good. Are you busy this morning?"

"Only work. Why?"

"Do you think you can take me to my appointments today? Not sure I have much strength for getting around on my own."

"Uh, yeah. I could call off. But Aunty can't take you?"

"She's been helping me too much lately."

"No problem, Mom. I have sick hours. When does your appointment start?"

"I need to check in by eleven."

"Westwood?"

"UCLA. Yes. But take your time."

"Let me call my job. I'll be over there by nine thirty."

"Okay, son. See you."

Shit.

I do have the hours. There is really no issue in accompanying Mom to her new oncologist. I just wish it were under better circumstances. That it's less of a surprise she isn't feeling well. But that is who she is. She carries a load of pain and sickness way more than she needs to.

I can still do things as she gets screened. I'll bring my work stuff, just in case. But I'll probably need to pay attention.

You would think a career nurse would be more attentive to her information being read if she were the patient. But I can't imagine being so close to dying and needing to deal with being unwell on a daily basis. 'Distraction' only starts to come close to the constant reality.

No time to make lunch. Guess I will have to go against my budget and get something next to the hospital. Those food trucks always looked pretty good.

Just hope I have the stomach to eat. Even though, on days like today, I can't manage to. There has to be good news waiting for Mom at the hospital. Being in between treatment programs has been hellish on her.

"That eye exam felt like a waste of time, didn't it?"

"This treatment always affects people in weird ways. They're just making sure your vision won't be impacted after you start."

"Isn't that something?"

"More than I'll know. You okay, Mom?"

"I'm fine. Let's make a stop here."

"You said Sister Ann was supposed to be calling you?"

"I'll call her back. I appreciate the prayer calls, but her timing has always been bad."

"You need some water?"

"I need the restroom."

"I'll wait here."

"Aren't you going to help me?"

"What?"

"Gotcha. Don't be so on edge."

"Funny, Mom. Go use it. And we'll go to the next appointment."

Thank God Mom still has a sense of humor. She seems to be holding together. This place can drain the life out of you.

But she is getting herself right. The least I can do is keep her company. There will be better days than this.

"Back already?"

"What did you think I was doing in there?"

"I guess you had the place all to yourself."

"Think you can find a wheelchair?"

"Are you having trouble walking?"

"I can get around. Just this damn fluid in me. Gets me winded real quick."

"There has to be one around here."

"Take your time and go find one. We'll get to the next appointment just fine."

"You're getting drained next, right?"

"Should be easier to get around after that."

"We'll use the wheelchair as long as we need to."

"Have you eaten since morning?"

"Had some cereal before I headed over."

"You'll be hungry soon."

"I'll be fine. I'll just grab food from the cafeteria or something."

"That's gonna be expensive."

"Don't mind paying. We're here for you, Mom. Let me go track down some wheels."

I had not quite done it before. Helped her out like this. Months ago, she was in much better shape.

We were somewhere smaller for her treatment, earlier in the year. She told me where to go. Torrance.

She had more life to her. More weight. She was definitely worse off only seven months later. But that's why we're here. The qualification screening better work. She has made it this far, but she doesn't have many options left.

She will get whatever she needs from me.

ULTRASOUND ABDOMINAL PARACENTESIS

"YOU FEELING BETTER?"

"It's easier to breathe. Feels better to move around."

"That was a lot inside of you."

"Three liters…have mercy."

"Is it a different color every time?"

"It's usually yellow or a greenish color."

"Like slime?"

"It was gray once. That was pretty strange."

"What do they mean?"

"The different colors?" Not much. It can change depending on what medication you're taking. But fluid is fluid and whatever it looks like, it needs to come out of me."

"I'm sure you're relieved you no longer have much inside of you."

"I hope it doesn't come back."

"The nurse felt confident you weren't getting any more."

It's not up to her. We'll see what the doctor says after I restart chemo."

"You're all done for the day. Did you still want to— where did you want to go?"

"The spicy Chinese chicken."

"And it's not kung pao chicken?"

"What's that?"

"The spicy chicken you want."

"That's not it."

"General Tsao's?"

"What are all these names? No, it's fried and pepper-like."

"Do you get hungry normally, after you're drained?"

"Like, I got the fluid removed so I must have a lot of empty space to fill with food?"

"Something like that. Does it feel like you're missing something?"

"It tends to feel like I have too much of it, needing to get chemo and get drained like this."

"That place you want to get the spicy chicken from, is it near the house?"

"You know it. We went there all the time when you were little."

"Clean Fast Slauson Wok? That place is still open?"

"They're in good shape. As far as I know. The people there will be happy to see how you've grown so."

"I haven't eaten from there since the ninth grade."

"Let's go. You probably want to beat the evening traffic."

"That's alright. We'll get you some food, and by the time I head home, it should be easier to travel the freeways."

"Thanks for helping your mommy out today."

"It's what I'm supposed to do."

"I don't take it for granted. I know you have important things to be doing."

"None more important than giving you a hand."

"I just want to get well. It's been two years of this, out of nowhere."

"The doctor feels really good about this next round."

"Hope it does the trick."

"Does Slauson Wok still have the Louisiana Famous Fried Chicken extension?"

"It never tasted the same."

"Hits the spot though."

"These drugs have killed any taste for food I can have. On the rare occasion I do crave something, I got to try and see if the food can go down decently."

"Then we'll do it."

"Let me get the car. You hang here."

"Where else will I go?"

CBC AND AUTO DIFFERENTIAL

"YOU SURE YOU'RE ALLOWED TO eat this stuff?"

"The doctor said I couldn't not eat it."

"I don't know if that's the best answer, Mom."

"I don't have that kind of cancer. Where I need to stay away from certain things."

"Just want to make sure we aren't making things worse."

"More than what I have going on already? Impossible."

"You are gaining some healthy weight back."

"I'm in the mood for something to taste good."

"There are plenty of other things that can do that, besides Jack in the Box."

"It happens to be what I'm feeling today. I have to follow the craving, or else I won't eat much."

"How come you don't crave smoothies or wraps?"

"I eat enough of that vanilla food at the treatment center. And Lord knows I can use something right now that does not require an obscene amount of hot sauce."

That's how I know she'll be okay. She can still complain about how tasteless the hospital food is.

"Those doctor folks up in there are killing me more than the tumors."

Mom's a few weeks into her new treatment program. She checks in and gets her bloodwork done. It gets processed, and then she can start with the chemotherapy. I can't imagine what it feels like. Pumping that druggy goo into your system.

She said she doesn't feel anything in the moment. No real pain or discomfort. But you can't talk to her in that state. She gets sluggish. Sleepy, even. A blessing the intake process isn't any more volatile.

I accompanied her the first few times. She does it every week now. Fridays.

Quickly, she insisted I stop taking her. She wasn't driving herself around much anymore. The chemo, pain, and medication made operating a vehicle too worrisome a task. She would find her way there but didn't mind if I picked her up once in a while, to keep her company on the hard days.

It's weird. In what feels like ancient times, when I was a kid, the end of the school week had a much different cadence to it. From pre-school, through most of elementary, I couldn't wait to see my mom picking me up in the afternoons. Because it meant my fast food treat for the week was on its way. Fries, orange soda, and a toy from somewhere.

Now I pick her up and take her where ever she wants to go, to start the weekend off. Telling her, as she told me, there's more to food than the drive-thru window. But we'd end up there anyway. Out of love. And it was just easier.

"You wanted this so much, you didn't think about what you were going to order?"

"I haven't been in this kind of line in ages. Why are there three menu boards?"

"They give you the first so you can figure out what you want before you get to the real one. So you don't hold up the line. The second is just for promos."

"Doesn't help."

"You like breakfast. It'll be something different."

"They still serve breakfast at five in the evening?"

"All day."

"Then gimme the Grande Sausage burrito, with the salsa on the side. Small coffee. Two cream. One sugar."

"Guess you knew all along."

"Just needed to see it, I suppose."

COMPLETE BLOOD COUNT

"I CAN'T BELIEVE THIS WAS what the fuss was about."

"You don't think it's good?"

"It's fine. But that's the problem. It's just a really fine burger. Why are cars always wrapped around the corner? For this?"

"A perfectly adequate hamburger is hard to come by these days. You get plenty of fresh ingredients, and you just want a reliable burger that is a good sum of those ingredients."

"I can't even say that, for these prices, you could get three of the same entrée at Burger King. They're more expensive than anything here."

"Times have changed, Mom. Restaurants have to pay more, so we pay more."

She's now a month and a half in. A bit of the same. She isn't feeling terrible pain anymore. Her default now is that she has cancer, and it makes her feel funny, with infrequent instances of affliction. On account of the chemo doing its job. Hopefully.

Her appearance has changed. Hair's gone. Bald as the day she came into this world. She probably had more hair back then. I'm taking her on a wig and beanie shopping spree tomorrow.

The chemo has also darkened her extremities – blackened her palms, tongue, and toes. She says it's strictly cosmetic. No torment associated with it.

She got on me about that the other day. Asking every minute if something was hurting. I just feel like I can't take any chances. She certainly can't afford to. The stakes are way too high. But she assured me she would tell me if something felt any more wrong than it already did.

Being sick or being healthy, she still had the means to live. And she was more than grateful she could stand on her own two feet to tell me to ease up. So I have.

"I think I know why they call it In And Out."

"They just leave the N in the middle, Mom."

"Oh, whatever. They have a restroom? Food's ready to go."

"Over there, behind the drinks."

"How do you eat this stuff?"

"You're the only person I know that doesn't sit well with the burgers."

"Must have been those fries."

"You wanted them well-done."

"Yours sure didn't look it."

"They taste better with the sauce and onions and cheese."

"I'll keep that in mind when I'm far away from this place."

"Well, now you know. You have to have at least one Double Double before you die – op, sorry."

"I told you to quit with that word around me, son."

"I just didn't mean to suggest—"

"Whether it's this blasted thing inside of me or old age, I will be gone one day."

"It'll be a good while from now."

"We know."

"Go to the restroom. You'll enjoy their shakes. Everybody loves their shakes. We'll get some for the road."

"I'll scratch it off the bucket list."

DIFFERENTIAL AUTOMATED

"NO, THERE ARE A BUNCH of trucks around LA."

"And they all serve the things you would eat at a sit-down restaurant, just in small trays?"

"More or less. You can get something a little different than tacos or burgers or sandwiches, and still kind of be on the go."

"Seems like a good way to charge you more for the same food at a real restaurant."

"Keeping up a building is expensive, Mom. People can serve the food they love, just in a cheaper way that still gets them good exposure."

"Long as you're paying."

"Yeah. I got it, Mom."

"You better not be paying fifteen and eighteen dollars for food at that fancy place you work at."

"Naw. Twice a week."

"That's too much, Jay!"

"I meant the office covers one lunch a week. Kind of our treat for getting work done. And then I'll usually pay for another lunch myself."

"Even once a week…"

"I'm still using the knapsack you got me at least three times, between Monday and Friday."

"Raised you right then. You can make a lot of this at home. And probably better."

"I try to grab food from the trucks that would be a little too busy to make on my own. That way, it feels like the extra charge was worth it."

"And all of these trucks are serving something different?"

"That's usually the idea. A lot of these trucks serve in packs. Seems easier to get some orders going if your food's set apart from the other trucks."

"How about that one?"

"The Peruvian barbecue truck?"

"I think that's the one that's smelling so good."

"Haven't had it myself. Let's try it out."

"Or what about that one?"

"They just do cupcakes in that one, Mom."

"Oh. Guess that's why the whole thing is pink."

"So you want to travel to Peru?"

"I don't know. I haven't had a hotdog, I think since you were a kid. But those hotlinks from that Southern comfort truck do look mighty good."

"We can do both. Get an item from the Peru truck, and the link truck, and share.

"No! Too much money."

"It's okay. We have time. Your clinic was so short."

"Doctor thinks I'm making good progress."

"Then let's celebrate, Mom. You earned it."

"Okay, get something nice from the link truck. You know I like everything on my hotdog. I'll be at the cupcake truck."

"You wanna split up?"

"Small as these rolling businesses are, they sure have large menus. Need time to decide how I want dessert."

"Ha. Alright. Don't wander off too much while you check out the other trucks."

CANCER ANTIGEN 125

"YOU OKAY, MOM?"

"I'm alive. Best I've got right now."

"Hope you aren't too discouraged by the news. The doctor says there are still some strong options left. And they're pulling out of this drug early to give you a head start on the next one."

"You said this place has a secret menu? What the heck is that? Why won't they just put it on the real menu?"

Here we are again. Back at the beginning, it feels like. I'm sure Mom is a sea of despair right now. We were really hoping for some good news.

Mom got her CAT scans done. Computed axial tomography. Honestly, it's scarier than the cancer.

Scans are medical report cards that tell you what kind of progress you're making, trying to beat whatever life-threatening disease is kicking your ass.

You get one at the start of your diagnosis. The CAT is the very test that contains the vital information. So in the modern medical world, it's one of the biggest advancements to let sick people know their lives are changed forever.

A more than helpful tool. But you hate it for existing.

In many ways, Mom would consider herself cancer-free, if she never looked at the scan results. If the doctor never told her what it all meant. But the initial scan saved her life. Stopped the suffering of the unknown, so the bodily healing wasn't so far behind.

It would be nice to go down an established course of treatment, and just keep doing it until she is well again.

Year one, the chemo had Mom mostly to her old self. She wasn't lying in a hospital bed, unable to do anything she never thought about not doing a couple of years ago.

The periodic scan, after the first, can affirm all the good signs that tumors are shrinking. But they can also show you the long road that remains.

Destinations generally had twists and turns to get to them. But very rarely did the journey include the words, 'progressive' and 'advanced stages.'

"It's a fun way to get some buzz going for the restaurant."

"But once you're here, how do you know what to order?"

"People tell you how to before you come in. Feels like a cool speak-easy thing that way."

"Those were illegal, dear son."

"The only crime here is never having tried the vegan Mac Daddy."

"Vegan?"

"Vegan. Trust me. You won't miss anything from the original Big Mac."

"I think I will if I'm eating a salad instead. This place isn't even McDonald's."

"No, vegan. It does include some roughage, but they rebuild the dish from the uh – table up, using plant-based products."

"So…a salad. With some shape to it."

"You're still going to have the bun, the patty, the cheese. It just won't be coming from any animals."

"And you're sure it's good?"

"I think you'll appreciate trying it at least, Mom. Though yes, I do love it."

"But you like meat."

"My salads don't have to have meat on them."

"Ah! It *is* a salad!"

"Mom. Please."

"Well…we're here. Might as well give it a shot. I don't know what all this other stuff on the regular menu is anyway."

URINALYSIS, DIPSTICK

"I THOUGHT THIS WAS SUPPOSED to be healthier than ice cream."

"It can be. But you can still go crazy."

"All those candy crumbs and brownie chunks don't look too healthy to me."

"You don't have to get those, Mom. They have plenty of fruit and nut options. Like a parfait."

"And you can put whatever you want, or however much you want in your cup?"

"That's the idea. TCBY."

"TCB – who?"

"The style of getting the treat. You can customize as much as you see fit to. But you also don't have to get any toppings. The flavor mixtures can feel like they're enough."

We are celebrating.

Mom had a certain sensation in her belly for a while. The identifiable dagger that tells us treatment isn't going the way it's supposed to, is her abdomen region. If it swells to distention, she's got fluid. An excess of it. Also means the current chemo regimen is no longer working, and will gradually lose more of its potency fighting Mom's cancer.

She calls up the doctor and requests an ultrasound. No fluid. Guess as long as she's been dealing with it, she gets some phantom agitation once in a while.

With the assurance that the new drugs are doing their job, we decided to mark the small good news with something sweet. Mom was also craving something cold and delightful so we had to do it. And she had never known the magic of frozen yogurt.

"It's good. Next time—"

"Next time? Thought this was too much. Too many sugary things."

"Your cup is too much. You got the large. Mixed just about every set of two flavors sharing a machine, and you top it off with cereal and gummy bears?"

"No dessert for me tonight."

"For the next month at least. My goodness."

"Ha. Okay, Mom."

"I see why you got the waters. Feels like I was eating crackers all of a sudden."

"That's how you know you're getting the real deal. A lot of frozen cream tends to irritate the throat."

"I like the yogurt up to that part."

"You just have to keep a bottle handy."

"So there are a bunch of these places around now, huh?"

"Pretty commonplace these days. You got 7-Elevens, Trader Joe's, Targets, and froyo, as far as the eye can see."

"Froyo…and that's what you're supposed to call it? That's what all the kids say?"

"It's mostly just the name now. Like cheese curls are just Cheetos."

"I still say cheese curls."

"Because you like little cousin Davey and Samantha not knowing at all what you're talking about."

"That, too."

"I'll take you to another one in Inglewood next time. Even crazier flavors and toppings. Just to see what it's like."

"Make sure they also have the plain, the strawberry, and chocolate. That's all anyone ever needs for sweet treats."

"Ever since I was a kid, you've always gone for Neapolitan."

"After a certain age, that's all that sweet things taste like. Those three."

COMPREHENSIVE METABOLIC PANEL

I'M STUFFED.

Mom says it felt good to be full of food again. Just food.

We went to a Brazilian steakhouse. Mom more than enjoyed herself.

It's crazy how many things I've done, being grown and out of Mom's protection. I've taken many things for granted. The things my friends and I do, without thinking much of them. The stuff that just so happens to make our lives a little more interesting and full of enough spontaneity – Mom had to miss out on.

She did plenty before getting sick. Did some traveling. Went on some adventures of her own. But for most of my life, even after I was out of the house, she was always busy working and providing.

We hadn't spoken a spit bubble's worth about her being sick, in any way, all evening. Felt like the old days. And it felt like they could occur again.

Before we went into the restaurant, we spent some time finding some parking. No spaces were available near the place. Mom was saying I could park a little further away, and she could handle the walking. But I didn't want to sour an already good night with her needing to take a break from walking, to catch her breath.

After circling the restaurant once, a spot opened up on the side. A good two-hundred feet from the restaurant, so minimal walking was required. Problem was, it was one of those curbs next to the pole with a million different parking signs attached. You can park here, but only during these hours, and with a permit – for an hour. Doesn't apply on Sundays. But it was very much a Thursday night.

It was after six, so we qualified for at least surviving one of the sign's rules. But we weren't sure if that negated the others. Then Mom remembered. She gave me her handicap placard.

That's what she called it. Because she always called it that. I told her people didn't quite call it that anymore, but she was right.

Early on, accompanying her to her appointments, she gave me the placard. Told me I shouldn't park in the provided parking garage because paying thirteen dollars every time felt like the worst crime to commit on yourself.

The blue token of sorts safeguarded cars from paying any kind of fees at parking meters, or from adhering to most signage – eliminating the risk of getting a ticket.

It also got a lot of usage when Mom wasn't in the car as well. But I somehow forgot about it that night. And Mom came to the rescue.

We gave it a try. We were mostly convinced it should have worked. I placed it around the neck of the rearview mirror, and we went about our evening.

I thought that stupid parking sign was going to be on my mind for all of dinner. But the momentary return to a normal outing with Mom made me forget my concerns instantly.

It didn't take much. Laughing. Reminiscing. There was wisdom; an exchange between generations – parent and child, over a meal.

We finished the perpetual feast of cuts of steak and pork, and eventually returned to the car. Waddled, was more like it.

No ticket.

Mom was more overjoyed than I was. Her happiness and lack of sickness, at that moment, truly made my night.

I had to be mindful to celebrate the good days with her. In front of her and away from her.

We did not know what would happen with her greatest fight, even two weeks from then. But the evening was enough to make us smile, without thinking of much else.

Cancer doesn't care how hard you try to get rid of it. It can still have its way.

And we can still have our victories.

THE GIANT KILLER

AS FAR AS LITTLE ROBERT was concerned, Christmas came several times a year. The feeling of the holiday.

It was the anticipation of something too great to fathom, all hours of the night. He always felt compelled to rest for the thing he thought would be the equivalent of being a step into the afterlife.

Most of the dimensions of this before-Christmas feeling also occurred during social events with family. A birthday party at a family-fun center. A function at a huge park.

That day, he was going to go to Six Flags Magic Mountain for the first time. He could not wait to fly up and down the tracks on the rides.

In the grand scheme of traveling in packs with his extended family, his cousins and aunts and uncles, the experiences were always additional chances for non-home food.

Some might look upon little Robert and gather he was not a light kid. He was healthy. His mom always spoke to a special person at the department store for his husky pants. The child was overweight, but he never had any issues getting on anything or fitting into any adventure.

Suffice it to say little Rob had an appetite where ever he went. And as a nine-year-old, who never skipped a homemade meal in his house, he jumped at any occasion to expand his world and eat fast food – or food from any restaurant.

His parents did not believe in eating out often. So much so, even a hot and ready pepperoni slice from the gas station express bar was a rare treat to indulge Robert's senses in.

A friend, who went out to theme parks more often than Rob, told him how spellbinding the grounds were – eating food you were hungry to consume after every ride. And that the sustenance was indeed available every fifty feet or so.

The coaster parks were places where you could only get certain types of food. But most of the parks carried hotdogs and hamburgers and fries and pizza and popcorn, and cotton candy. Robert was excited to receive the park's version of those entrées, understanding every place served the staples up a little differently.

Above all, the boy was attentive to hearing of the sweetest park creations – rods of fried dough people called churros. And strange donut cakes that looked like a bed of French fries, stuck together. They were covered in powdered sugar, and some even had chocolate syrup with ice cream on top. Funnel cake.

At the top of the treat food chain was an alleged sweet and sour snack the locals knew too well. A giant pickle, bigger than Rob could imagine – according to his friend – that was stuffed with fruit-flavored candy. The kind of candy he was only allowed to savor on Valentine's Day, on Halloween, and his birthday, if he did not beg for his presents too much. The pickle would be stacked to bursting with Skittles and Starbursts and Now-and-Laters. The devilish refreshment went by many names, but it was the pinnacle of exclusive park foods – reserved only for its action-oriented patrons.

Robert was sure the delectable snacks were the perfect version of the Leimert Park flea market food that teased him whenever he accompanied his mother to the theme park for small businesses. A strictly smell-but-not-buy situation. An easy no-go from the parental unit.

The boy would never spend all day at the flea. Though it often felt that way, before his mother decided she was done shopping. They were certainly going to spend more than a few hours at Six Flags to get their money's worth for the trip. And they most certainly were not going to just sniff the air and starve.

Food was going to be had at the place Robert was sure he would have the most fun at for a lifetime. And a dazzling snack or two, between meals, if he was on his best behavior.

The Saturday like no other came. He got up on his father's first call to wake and get out of bed, instead of the usual third. Breakfast was a surprise change of pace from the sugary cereal Robert was allowed to have once a week. He would always prefer a hot dish. And that morning, the bacon, eggs, and toast – with cantaloupe – was a welcomed shift of the routine. Even his parents knew it was a special day, somewhere in their high-up adult hearts. The boy kept his composure and ate his morning meal with the quiet happiness of knowing the best was yet to come.

Unbeknownst to little Robert, the meal was a peace offering for an inhumane number of rude awakenings the day would contain. The strength from the hot breakfast would barely be enough to maintain his childish sanity.

From the moment Robert's family caravan crossed into the driveway and parking lot of the amusement park, it was clear there was a social code of conduct that resulted from what customers could afford or were willing to pay for.

You could see some of the park's biggest, most thrilling coasters from the drive up. That did not stop a good number of patrons, Rob's family included, from driving what felt like miles from the sighting near the entrance. Every fifty or so yards, hundreds of people walked up to the park gates. It was not like there was no parking available up front, but the signage indicated it was for customers who valued convenience more than twenty extra dollars.

The group of cars finally stopped. They were not on cement anymore, with painted lines guiding where to drive, or indicating how far to park from the other car next to yours. They were in a gravel lot. Nondescript. Near a buzzing contraption that looked like it helped with the park's electric power.

Parking attendants were not even present to direct traffic this far. They sent you to a distant land governed by orange traffic cones. Dirty ones, at that. Probably from all the dust the cars were rolling up, as the rocks underneath slid under the cars' tire pressure.

There were no cool signposts and watchtowers either. The ones adorned with row numbers, and a cartoon character, to help you remember where you left your vehicle – in a concrete sea of automobiles. They got none of that. Only Uncle Thomas' bright red Miata that was too small for his family of three, and carried an annoying car alarm to the tune of Baby Got Back. So perhaps the family in attendance dodged a bullet for the long return to their cars, through the entire lot. The Miata would just do its best Sir Mix-a-Lot impression if the party got lost.

Everyone got out of their vehicles. Aunty Sherry insisted all the kids crowd around her to get their dose of sunscreen spray. And it did not matter that they were all black. Safety did not care what color you were.

The other adults huddled together to discuss something. Little Rob could not understand what was so hard about getting everyone to march towards the park.

Short of the spray-down, the meeting amongst the parents took nearly ten minutes. They were doing some serious math. No one else seemed to be bothered.

The next thing little Robert saw was his dad and Uncle Herb lifting a massive blue cooler from the trunk of Aunty Rose's car. The one she let all the kids slap a sticker on once a year, so there was only a little blue surface left.

That big cooler was usually a harbinger of great things. Rob was not sure if it was established among her brothers and sisters, but Aunty Rose could cook. She was the best. She was the main family member cooking for all the barbecues and end-of-year holidays.

The family started walking towards the front of the park, like everyone else, away from the fences of the gravel lot. Immediately, the leading adults veered away from the clearly established route to the gates. Little Rob's eyes tried to beat the group's feet to the destination. There was another path they were starting down. The end of which had trees and benches, and other frugal families that believed in saving every last penny for God knew what for. They were headed towards a picnic area. They were going to eat before enjoying the wickedly sweet treasures of the park. Probably no treats at all!

It was an early lunch for a Saturday. Only two-and-a-half hours before, little Rob was getting the chomp just right on his bacon and was swishing through his pillowy eggs with his buttered toast. He even had enough on his plate, before asking for seconds, to make an open-faced sandwich with the remaining bacon, eggs, and toast. That was always the boy's perfect bite. If he could stack it or drag a piece of bread across his plate to grab the very last bit of everything, the next few hours were always going to be alright.

Except for when they were not.

Things most assuredly were not – as everyone set up camp with blankets and plasticware on a grassy knoll, in the middle of the fancy, marked lot. The family was far off to the side of the miniature park, with a picturesque view of the rollercoasters in front of the traveling unit. You could hear the tracks in use and the happy customers screaming their heads loose.

"Slow down."

"It's good."

"You'll choke, Robbie."

"But—"

"You can enjoy your food without trying to win an imaginary eating contest. There is no prize, I promise you."

"I just want to make sure I won't hold us up when it's time to leave."

"If you end up choking or vomiting, you'll hold us up anyway. And we probably couldn't do the rides at all," little Robert's mom smirked. Knowing she had her son cornered in his eager logic. He was always caught between wanting to do something – for fear that he would never be able to do it again – and needing to do something else.

Perpetual curses. The boy was sure of it in his little bones.

But the food was good. Cold fried chicken, rolls, and potato salad. Chips and pouched juice on the side.

Eating the chicken at that temperature was a first. The entrée was not cooled, as if Aunty Rose fried it up and let the chicken sit out before packing it and driving it over. It tasted like it was prepared recently and sat in the fridge at least for one night. Sitting in the cooler kept it chilled, but not as cold as taking leftovers from a fridge that needed to be reheated.

The grease was the ex-factor. It kept the chicken flavorful, even without the crunch of being freshly cooked. And little Rob lived for that crunch of chicken, however subtle it might have been.

The bird did taste different, but not any worse than the hot counterpart. Almost like cold versus melted cheese. The temperature was a crucial factor, but the alternative had its benefits.

Cold fried chicken almost had paper-like skin. The remaining batter was more at risk of falling off after every bite. But little Robert could taste more of the seasoning of both the skin and the meat while the dish was cold. A much more thorough venture for the tastebuds, even if hot fried chicken was still the preferred confrontation with the senses.

It scored major impression points for trying cold pizza one day. Little Rob was still on the fence about that one.

The picnic to curb the cravings, and the money spending while inside the mountain of magic, was still the enemy. But the food did its job. It calmed the boy down, filling him with a certain satisfaction only Aunty Rose's food could do. He was going to get something to eat in the park somehow. The early lunch just helped him gather himself for hardening his resolve to obtain the treats.

The family wrapped their meal, after what was beginning to feel like an unusual version of timeout. Especially after little Rob finished his food and was told not to eat any more than the plate and a half he had had.

The boy had to try the cold experiment out with different pieces of chicken. He had gotten through two legs and a wing. He was about to reach for a thigh when his mother gave him the look to cease.

Another stretch of infinite asphalt later, the family was in front of the amusement park. The colors, the height of it all – little Robert could hear music in the air. See the characters from TV, alive and in person, greeting guests. Though there was a decent amount of distance between Rob, his folks, and the other side of the entry gate – which meant they would have been officially in the park and able to do whatever they pleased.

The closer the family got to scooching through the turnstiles and crossing the threshold to their Saturday destinies, the clearer the music had become. The characters became more visible, and the perky parky employees who looked no older than Rob's oldest teenage cousins in attendance.

And the smells – it was a flea market of food vendors. He got generous whiffs of the frying dough. The sugar. The popcorn. It was only accented perfectly by the curious sounds of rollercoaster cars racing up and down their tracks.

Everyone else got in the spirit of attending the park the closer the entrance got. The chatter of what was going to be ridden and conquered was at a crescendo.

"You want to ride Goliath with me?"

"Sorry, cousin Robert. I'm going to split with the big kids. But maybe I'll catch you on there."

"I am a big kid!"

"You are, cuz, but you'll have more fun with Trevor and Tiff."

The kids who were always doing their own thing – in the coolest way – at all the family functions, charged off with the swagger of the Mighty Morphin' Power Rangers in a music video. And the Power Rangers were certifiably little Robert's heroes.

"Dad, where are they going? Can I go with them?"

"You will just slow them down, buddy. You'll do better to hang with us."

The boy's worst fears were realized. All who were left were the adults and the twins. Trevor and Tiffany. Always whining. Never sharing their toys. Always getting into fights with each other.

"But we can still do Goliath and the big rides, right?"

"We may. But you might be too small. Let's see how Bugs Bunny Land goes."

It was obviously the name for a version of the park that was not the best the magic mountain had to offer. It sounded like a place for little kids.

Little Rob was devastated. He was in the easy group. Convenient walking, and in no rush to do anything. The group that was too okay with doing however much they were able to get to, before eventually getting tired – from zero thrills – and calling it a day. The boy had to do something before he had no treats and no big kid excitement.

The place he knew was going to change his life was not going to turn into a prison sentence.

The remaining family made their way to the place at the park where little kids should not have felt left out. The torture of the walk was that it was on the way to the attraction little Rob vowed to ride at least once while in attendance. Goliath.

You could see the blue scaffolding and the orange tracks as you approached the children's sector. He had to find a way. The boy's mother would be too concerned about his safety, knowing full well his present situation was always going to be the outcome – from a full breakfast and a begrudgingly pleasant lunch.

His father would be a good target to convince, given their conversation a moment ago. But he seemed more involved with his wife. You could not tear them apart in public – ever the cutest couple.

"Trevor. Do you really want to ride these baby rides?"

"They don't seem so bad."

"But don't you want to do the high and fast ones?"

"The ball pit place looks cool. It has a ball gun!"

Hopeless. They would be done with everything in an hour. With the number of people that poured in by the time the family entered the park, those sixty minutes would have been precious time lost to wait in a much more important line for a worthy coaster.

Little Rob would play along. He would go on all the biggest rides within the Bugs Bunny minipark that he could more than stomach. He would also work on Trevor. Asking to go on a big kid attraction in numbers would help.

One ride later, two rides – three – if you count the ball house that Trevor nearly threw a kiddie fit over to get inside of, Robert was itching for an opening. He had to effectively put it in his parents' minds that he was ready for something in which you could not see the entire queue or crowd when you got in the rollercoaster car.

That was when cousin Willem showed up.

He was not with the party at the beginning. He worked nights and must have told everyone he would catch up once he got some sleep.

Willem was in an age group all his own. Not quite one of the adults, but he definitely was not in the little kid pool. And he was too old for the big kids, who were off on their adventure, worlds away from the basic birthday party little Rob was stuck in.

He was closer to the aunts and uncles, and the boy's parents, always choosing to hang with them at the dinner gatherings. For whatever reason, little Robert could not fathom.

Miraculously, he showed up with two churros in his hands. The second, no doubt, for his favorite little cousin who would soon express interest.

"You gonna eat both of those, Will?"

"Figured you could use a snack. The cart by the entrance just put these fresh ones out, and I couldn't resist. You interested?"

Little Robert could not answer such a question, from fear he would get his parents arrested – the way he wanted to scream his affirmative.

"Now you know that is too much for him to have," Rob's mother interrupted.

"Sorry, Aunty Pam. Should've squared it with you first."

"Trevor! Tiffany!"

The twins saw Willem and what he was holding. They stopped bickering about whatever their current conflict was and ran over. Puny dogs that saw an outstretched hand with treats in it.

"Split it amongst the three of them, so we don't have to deal with overdosed kids later," Rob's mom explained.

"Sure, Aunty. Lemme just—"

And then Willem, in all of his grownup authority, with the will to do whatever he wanted – because he had some money to spend on whatever he liked – finished the last couple of inches of his whole churro. Cinnamon sugar dust fell from what appeared to be a satisfying final bite of an edible dynamite stick that exploded the senses. And as if little Rob needed further confirmation, Will licked his index finger and thumb to make sure he got the very last of the magic food.

"You heard Aunty Pam. I'll try to be as even as I can."

It was likely that, after declaring such a cautious approach, the judge carrying out the fair splitting of resources would either break more than a third, or a bit less. The boy was betting on the latter.

"Don't be afraid to give me a little more, cousin. I can handle it. It's going to make the twins fight more than they already do," little Rob confided in his relative, hoping to sweeten the deal of his portion.

"I hear you, little Rob. Gonna just…"

And in a move of supreme tone-deafness, Willem split the churro with what he understood as his best effort. It was a privileged point of view because he probably had had a hundred churros in his life so far.

The man butchered the poor snack. He overcompensated for not gripping the sugared rod directly, trying to be clean and neat by using the wax paper guard to divide. Then he viewed the three pieces, two visibly bigger than the third portion, and he gave the larger ones to Trevor and Tiffany. The least deserving twins on the planet.

"Hmm, must've taken a little extra off this last bit, but not by much. Here you go, cousin. Still packs the flavor of a full churro."

Easy for him to say, with residue from his full churro still on his cheeks.

No matter. Though the boy's soul was filled with a certain kind of angst he had never known, he possessed it. In his hands was one of the charms of the magic mountain. Still warm. Still littering the pavement, and his hand, with excess cinnamon sugar dust. A special kind of dirty little Rob was grateful to get filthy in.

He wasted no time. The boy took a bite, noting the instant parallel to the Cinnamon Toast Crunch cereal. The forbidden breakfast his parents only let him enjoy twice a year. It was perfect enough on its own, being eaten between cold and room temperature – because of the milk.

The churro was cereal, come to life; a loaf, uncut and unsliced into bite-sized squares. It was a cinnamon bun that was crusted over. Still soft to the touch but existing more like a fancy chip. It would change little Robert's life forever. At least, that's how he felt. He would share it with anyone whose life was so miserable, without the injecting of the sugary sweet light that radiated from the churro.

Before he knew it, the boy's small bit of paradise was no more. There was a quick-setting melancholy that resulted from little Rob's tingling taste buds being without, but the snack gave him something he did not have minutes ago. The wherewithal to see himself atop one of the greatest heights the magic mountain had to offer – riding on the shoulder of the Philistine giant.

"Mama, do you think cousin Willem can take me on Goliath? I've already been on everything here."

"You won't quit about that ride, will you?"

"Willem probably wants to ride it, too. Right?" the boy asked his relative, not trying to sound too earnest in his pursuit.

"Yeah, sure. Rob seems too big for this little league stuff anyway. I can give him a taste of the tween life."

"You sure he won't be a bother?" Pam asked.

"Naw, we'll ride it and come back."

"Don't give your cousin a hard time," little Rob's mother warned him.

"I'll be good."

"Then have fun, you two."

Little Robert was soon holding hands with Willem, headed off on a new quest to slay the behemoth of anticipation.

"Alright, cuz. Just you and me. Maybe we'll sneak in two rides. Say that the line for Goliath was just long. What do you think?"

The boy smiled and nodded with an enthusiasm he, at last, felt free to express.

"And if you get hungry at any time between rides, don't let me stop you," Rob insisted.

* * *

END OF THE DAY.

The big kids had ridden all they could. The twins were at their fussiest. The next move was half of a surprise, and the other half was just the best the parents could do after a long nine hours of organized fun. Everyone was tired and in need of real sustenance before parting for their homes.

Denny's. It was just off the freeway, near the park.

The family left the mountain of magic a few hours before closing, so there were no crowds to keep the party of twelve from sitting together at the restaurant.

Little Rob was just as exhausted as the adults, having had a terrible afternoon. Willem was supposed to be his ace, his key to the kingdom of permitted abandon to the rest of the park – the way a big kid was supposed to enjoy the rides and food, and everything else the place had to offer. But Willem turned out to be a dud.

The two waited in line for forty-five minutes. More than enough time to brim with excitement over the commitment to see Goliath through, to see what the monstrosity had to offer.

The two got to the top of the loading station. The boy could see the rollercoaster cars and the attendants preparing the riders for their trip through the air.

The biggest problem little Robert thought he would have had to deal with was fulfilling the height requirement for the attraction. He was not quite at the forty-eight inches needed, but Willem assured him that an accompanying adult would smooth over his shortcoming.

Their turn was painfully close. The boy was keeping it cool. He allowed his mind to take him through the coaster, to the furthest reaches of the heavens – just outside of the open space on tracks – where cars full of people disappeared on their minute and seconds-long excursion of daring drops and gravity-force embankments.

Little Robert also paid close attention to the faces of the people who had gone and returned, the closer he got to boarding. Most seemed to be riding in an ordinary car at the start, either being on their best behavior or brushing with familiar territory. But a fair number of passengers, on the completion of their coaster lap, brandished wide grins and wind-tousled hair. They leaped out of their cars with renewed energy, having raced from a giant's point of view the attraction was supposed to inspire.

"You okay, cousin Will?"

"What?"

"You look like you have a mean stomachache."

"I'm fine. Just ready to get this thing over with."

The boy's adult relative was sporting a look of mild dread. Like a kid waiting in front of his school for his mom to pick him up in the afternoon, and she was late. So the kid began to worry about where she was. If she was okay. And ultimately, if he was going to get picked up.

The time came. They were positioned to take their seats towards the back. In the middle, between the actual center of the entire vessel, and the end of it.

The attendant gave the boy a questioning look, his height being a noticeable disqualification from riding. But she noted Willem and moved along.

The gate to little Robert's destiny opened, and he and his cousin got into their car. Their special car. The boy could feel it. The warm seat from the bottom that occupied the space not a few seconds ago. The restraints, a little dusty from the outside air, but critical in maintaining that the view from the heavens remained that way until they were back where mortals treaded.

They strapped themselves in. He would have squealed at that point, but Willem looked to be ready to collapse. It did not dissolve the boy's spirit for being so close to experiencing the peak of big kid activities.

As the attendant walked down Willem's side to double-check the restraints –

"Excuse me. I need to get off."

"Sorry, sir?"

"I need to get off. I can't ride this thing. Think I'm going to be sick."

"You're already strapped in."

"No, I must get off," Willem repeated, panic creeping in, betraying his best efforts to keep his voice calm and below a certain volume.

"Cousin Will, what's wrong?" the boy asked, unsure of what was happening. He was not fully mindful of the implications of his adult kin needing to get out of the car.

The one thing that seemed very unnatural was wanting off of an attraction that promised a taste of the magic feeling. Willem seemed fine the entire time until they entered the onboarding station.

The attendants did not seem to like the reversal much. The employee – looking like a young woman in high school – gave the grown man a mildly annoyed look and signaled to the operator at the ride controls. He pressed a button and all the lap restraints on the car loosened. Willem briskly lifted his like he was in a plane that was about to crash and burn. Little did his companion know that he had to be the parachute.

"I hope you feel better, cousin Will. I'll see you at the bottom," the boy promised, as he lowered his lap bar to prepare for takeoff.

"Sorry, but you're outside of the height requirements for this ride, little dude."

"But I'm already on."

"You have to be with an adult. We're going to have to let you off as well. Maybe try coming with someone else next time."

Little Rob could not bear to look around at the people witnessing the scene he was caught in.

"Let's just get out of here, buddy," Willem mostly begged, extending a hand to help little Rob out of the car. "I'll make it up to you."

The boy was astonished. He got the closest he could to riding with a giant, and he could not. The way his cousin's plain voice was returning, a desperate but real attempt, Rob sensed something else was happening.

It was a quiet, long walk back down to the dazzling, but graying scenery and passerby of the park below. Little Rob's dream had been dashed, stricken in spirit-breaking fashion.

"Are you okay now, cousin Willem?"

"Thanks for doing that, little man. I know how much you wanted to do Goliath. But I'm afraid of heights."

"Why did you agree to take me here then?" Rob frowned.

"Thought I could suck it up, but I'm a chicken. I am prepared to earn your forgiveness."

"Can we try another ride?"

"From the looks of these skyscrapers, I'll be happier down here."

"Oh," the boy returned, convinced his day was officially over.

"But we can do another thing. If you promise not to mention to the rest of the fam how I wussed out."

"What's that?"

"Ever had Dippin' Dots? The ice cream that comes in little orbs of different flavors?"

"No."

"Then how about I get you your first cup, the cup you don't have to share with anyone else, and we take a lap around this place to enjoy the views?"

"Deal!"

It was the least his cousin could do for his cowardly move.

The frozen treat was a revelation. Especially his banana sundae flavor. Ice cream that melted in his mouth from an unconventional shape, just to be familiar-feeling ice cream again – it did lift the boy's spirits. Though circling the attractions at the park was a maddening trip. So the talk of dinner out with his family, once they reunited, was a welcome change of pace. And the boy was determined to make it a worthwhile visit.

"You can't eat all that, baby."

"I'll try my best."

"You're going to let your son have that great, big thing? It's like eating an entire pizza. I told you he should have gotten something from the kid's menu."

The boy's father marveled at the dish placed in front of his son. A lot of the other family members also fondly considered the massive beef nachos plate. It appeared little Robert made the right choice.

"Let the boy have his fun with dinner. Seems like he earned it today," Rob's dad added, stealing a chip just on the outside of the toppings on the tray.

"What he doesn't eat, I can surely finish."

The boy silently resented the early concession on his behalf. It was a matter of perspective. He had never had the approximate freedom to order what he would envy on other people's plates whenever he and his family went out.

The Grande Texan Nacho Poncho at Denny's was essentially the thing he could get away with ordering from an ice cream truck. But assuredly, the portion made it an adult entrée.

"Now I'm sure you'll have fun giving this a whirl, buddy. But do you know the secret to eating more food than you're used to, if it's your mission?"

His father asked him like they were watching a basketball game, and the man was letting him in on a privileged secret of the sport.

"Try your darndest?"

"That's part of it. You'll probably get that bit down."

He grabbed the small plate that was served with the platter.

Oh, no. He was not going to divide the tremendous-looking mountain of chips and taco filling like he and his mom served his pancakes, was he?

Admittedly, Robert quite liked that parental move, as the syrup could soak the griddle cake a little more thoroughly. He still enjoyed some of the dry spots, to maintain the pancake's mass of various flavors and textures, but a large serving of nachos did not deserve the same treatment.

His father took a knife and brought the blade over a decent chunk of the dish, making to slide that much onto the appetizer plate.

"You just eat smaller bits of it. You polish it off. And sometimes, it'll even feel like you're getting a few helpings of the good stuff."

Little Rob, deflated a little, was relieved. If he were being honest, it was a lot of nachos. He got it because the picture told him he needed to order it. His parents, spent from the day, did not quite catch the order and allowed the waiter to record whatever came out of his mouth. And it sounded like reasonable food since they were hungry themselves.

When he said the name of the dish to himself, the meal sounded like a rollercoaster. The boy had not forgotten his vow. He was going to get on something that was perceived to be too big for him and ride it. Only, at the time of the Denny's visit, he was Goliath and the food was the rider. He was going to be in operation until every last crumb had had their turn accelerating – at full speed – to the thrilling darkness of the interior of his mouth.

"Don't forget to take some of the toppings for every bite. You don't want to fill up on dry chips."

"I know how to eat, Daddy."

"Well, excuse me. But maybe you could use a demonstration," the boy's dad responded, reaching for more of a covered nacho.

"No!" the boy said, laughing. "I can do it."

"Don't let me down, little Rob. Your mother already thinks you've bitten off more than you can chew before you've chowed down. Make me proud, son."

"He's eating a plate of food. He isn't on the shortlist for the Governor's Award," his mom said, dryly.

It was officially his duty. Everyone commenced dinner. Little Rob got to his. He picked up a chip that was weighed down with cheese, red sauce, and lettuce. He swiped it past a little taco meat, for solid measure. He grasped it firmly, the way his father showed him, like he had a stack of videogame cases in his hand, and he bit into his transition to big kid status.

It was a sophisticated loaded chip. The tortilla crisp was a little thinner, but wider – salted with something on the sour side, but it was hard to identify.

The cheese was not the usual runny paste he had known. It seemed so primal to the child then. The one he was consuming had a deep flavor to it. Peppery. He could see small green and red squares in it.

There was also the lettuce and the tomato chunks, the green salsa and sour cream – and little Robert usually did not care for the white topper – the zesty refried black beans, and the cilantro. Oh, the cilantro. It made the heavy plate of food feel a tad lighter to consume for an unknown reason. And to literally top it off, shredded cheese, that made the boy feel like he was eating food from a plate in a commercial. The kind that always had gooey cheese to put front and center – for the money shot – that should have sealed the deal for the product to be sought out and purchased.

Little Robert had endured so much at the mountain of magic to come to his dinner plate. It was always what he was after. He realized it at that very moment.

The family was conversing while eating, as they usually did. The restaurant was going about its usual business, but the boy was not attentive to any of it. He had been locked in a chamber with his dinner, the kind that limited the senses. You could hear voices, but could not discern any words.

Eating was a blissful, nonstop motion of a bite of nacho, or a few, and a tidying of the plate of whatever had fallen from the chips. Until the first half of little Rob's nacho platter was gone. He licked his greasy fingertips. Finished the last of his fries. The plate also came with fries, for some reason. Or he just thought people ordered fries with everything when they ate out. So that might have been the last thing the boy mentioned to the waiter before the staff member asked another what she wanted to eat.

The enamored child closed his eyes, grateful to have engorged himself in the manner he did. It was an incessant visceral affront to his tongue that had just been doused in ice-cold cola.

And then, battering into existence like it had been neglected for some time, the sensation of fullness rushed into the boy's view, as his surroundings came back into focus. But the second half of the platter was ready for its fateful departure.

He had had fun with the attraction he had only dreamt of until that evening. But he was ready to get off, with the eagerness of ten cousin Willems. He was fit to bursting. But Rob did not want to give his parents the satisfaction of telling him he was always going to hit a dead end on the road of what was supposed to be his special, magical adventure.

Little Robert needed a way to look triumphant. A way to show his parents he had things under control. And most importantly, that he had come to a more than acceptable stopping place, boldly going where no kid in his home had gone before.

"How's the food, son?" the boy's father checked in.

"Good. Just…is it okay if I— it's good."

WITH THE BOP AND THE BOIL

THE DAY WAS A DECENT one for Los Angeles. Nothing strange, from most points of view, since the sun was a good deal out. Martin Luther King Jr. Boulevard was wide as it was quiet, one Tuesday afternoon.

Clark's car was in the shop. The used car he had purchased from a friend's father's business had shown its real colors, being reliable, but it possessed the oddest aftermarket issues. The most bothersome defect was that he could not control the car alarm because he did not have a fob. So the car would cuss and yell and chirp at times – without any provocation. Thankfully, it would always turn off on its own. Eventually.

The man did his research. Read at least a dozen extended reviews. The auto shop where the car resided, for the time being, was the best place to take his vehicle. But even they could not discern base malfunction.

The owner of the repair garage had taken it as a personal challenge to figure out the problem.

So the car owner was not going anywhere for a few days. If he did not want to walk.

And Clark thought it best to have room to think with a walk that Tuesday, for the day was glorious. His life had changed with one critical admission to himself. The honesty illuminated a certain kind of try that had shined boldly in his gut for the day, so far.

But not getting anywhere fast enough was a royal pain. Mostly because he was in the hustle-at-200-miles-per-hour city, and he had wheels to operate but could not use.

Waiting on Uber or Lyft drivers was also painful, or whatever driver connected to an app that had a sign-up credit attached to it. The last thing Clark wanted to do was pay money for someone to take him somewhere, when he had a car he was about to pay at least an arm to fix. But it was okay.

Clark, a few years out of undergrad, with a job and an educational debt payment plan, knew what he wanted to head toward professionally. Or, put a little closer to the deep pangs of his soul, he had come to a place where he felt more than assured that he could go for it. Up against any manner of scrutiny.

But he still had a few things to consider and sift through. He wanted to get some of the critical details straightened out so they would generally feel good, down to the soles of his feet.

As a vague confirmation of the uprightness of his pathway, between MLK and Figueroa Street, a quaint liquor store sold his long-lost favorite flavor of Doritos. He could not find Black Pepper Jack for weeks after its initial run. He assumed its time had come because there was not enough demand to keep it on shelves.

He ignored the dust on the bag and purchased the perfect way to chew on his thoughts as they developed. Business owners – without much of their business – still needed their energy.

So there he was, on his mile-and-a-half-long journey. At the destination, he was going to meet a friend to tell her the good news. She offered to pick him up, but he said he would have been fine taking a stroll over.

If anyone bothered to pay attention, even a glance Clark could steal from some drivers keeping their eyes on the road, they might have seen him smile some. It was just him and his possessions – his phone, wallet, and house keys. And a grin that could not stop resurfacing from his snack habit.

He was not sure many people happened along the boulevard, just munching on chips. Plenty of people, most likely. But he felt like he was in a moment of heavenly opening. The way you could see the sun spotlight through rain clouds if you looked up at the right time.

Clark was in a body of water. That felt more like it. It was a running river of transition, and his boat was his favorite bag of seasoned tortilla triangles.

It felt like a commercial. And on TV, you never assumed the bag would go empty. You also never quite assumed the actor had somewhere else to be, though the years of programming rendered viewers to accept the reality-like universe at face value.

As a vessel for crossing over, the chips had to last. They just had to. To keep the vibe. To get Clark on his way. It would have been the golden sign that things would be okay.

So one chip at a time. The game was to savor and not inhale his new fortune.

In essence, he really enjoyed the act of collecting a bounty that had grown cold. Taking his time was how he got to the present situation in the first place.

It was going to be great and grand. Clark was certain there was a need for it where he lived. He respected the Starbuckses and the other cafes that did what they did. Even most fast-service restaurants that had WiFi did it, the ones that sheltered the unhoused trying to do something productive before they were thrown out.

There was a need for facilitation, for a co-working space, and he was going to provide that space to the dozen or so who needed it.

But Clark had to acquire ammunition. He knew after coming down from the high of clarity, the nagging concern for the logistics would surface. He crossed Broadway and considered what he had left in his bag after eating three chips. The first few were perfect, wholly shaped chips at the top of the bag, each crunch more satisfying than the previous one.

The serving suggestion was about twelve pieces, in a bag of around three or so servings. He was going to eat the whole thing and enjoy the salty snack down to the very crumbs of the crumbs. Completion was not the question. Getting to the other side of the river with limited propulsion was the thing to be done.

Clark had just crossed his second street when he noticed someone walking behind him. Not an uncommon occurrence on a Los Angeles sidewalk, in the middle of the afternoon. But not unlike the etiquette of the prototypical LA driver, it was usually a matter of whether or not the person behind was just trying to get where they needed to go, or was going to observe the various statutes of operating a death machine at lethal speeds as mere suggestions. Because in the city Clark loved like his father's cooking, people did not drive to get where they aimed to go. The vast majority only avoided close calls and accidents on the way to their many destinations. Not exactly solid navigation.

The shallow philosophizing brought him to the next matter. But before he could bring it about with another crunch of a Dorito, the stranger behind him got closer. And closer.

The distance between pedestrians was supposed to go without saying. Even in New York or in Tokyo, with the famous intersections of at least a hundred people passing along, no one was deliberately trying to crowd anyone else's space. The feet or so you did have, from leg to leg, became even more precious.

The two were nowhere near those eastward and far eastern conditions. There could have been a chance Clark was crowding up the middle of the curb, which would have been his bad. He had to allow for a passing lane, for others with a less leisurely gait. He moved over.

Still, the unidentified person – who could only be interpreted at that moment as a stalker – stayed behind the young man.

There was no not turning on the city in Clark. It was already plenty inside of him. The last resort was turning around to fully acknowledge he sensed someone was behind him and that he did not feel good about the positioning.

Clark went for it. But the intimate traveling companion already sidestepped from being behind and was alongside him.

"Nice bag of chips you got there."

"Thanks. It's been a long time coming. Finally got ahold of them."

"Hope you're taking your time then."

"Want one?"

"I believe in sharing the wealth. But I also believe certain gifts are one's own sometimes. You eat a few for my sake."

"I can surely do that."

"Would you like a wig?"

"Think I'm okay. Appreciate the offer to share in your riches as well."

"We'll take over the world. Your food expression with my fashion sense."

"That hot pink is striking enough for the both of us," Clark said.

"Magenta. But right on. Take care of yourself."

"You do the same."

The man wearing the wig, and holding a box full of wigs, walked on. He wore a dirty, beat-up backpack. His clothes looked as if he played golf hours before. But the sandals suggested he believed in comfort above many things.

The exchange somehow encouraged Clark to make sure he was going to do his job. It was the kind of confirmation that could only come before embarking to do something crazy, but the madness was going to work out in the end. Legally or not. Permits and zoning clearances notwithstanding.

The fresh fuel could not stop the questions, the funnel through which his excitement was tempered. He also had some big asks of his landlord.

Months ago, Clark rented a room in a house. It was supposed to be closer to something. He was not sure what. Neither was he sure about the arrangement in the Mid City neighborhood. He was not oblivious to the beyond expensive city he came from. The more than a handful of shared residences that were all over – people keeping makeshift quarters in living rooms to make rent every month. But it stemmed from the paradoxically wholesome grind to love where high-profile things happened and where people tried to make a name for themselves.

Clark's particular room existed within a home whose first family had long since made a run for further, more conservative residence communities around Palmdale. They figured they would hold on to the first house and lease it out to college kids and others who needed a place to stay.

Apparently, it belonged to another family after the first moved on. Then the rooms started to go to rent on an individual basis, on the assumption that adults could surely cohabitate in the space like any full-fledged apartment complex. Except there was a communal kitchen and a communal restroom. Utilities had to be shared, and the current occupants – or tenants – as Clark preferred, had to agree upon an efficient sanitization schedule with which to keep the home tidy.

Eventually, a fraternity called the place home base before they decided to move the hub somewhere else, or were forced out by the owner, slash landlord. And within a year of a slight remodeling and repair, Clark found his way into the fold.

His other two housemates were very grown adults and were out of the way. But given Clark's circumstances and credit score, he was able to snag the main bedroom of the household. A Godsend.

He had the biggest room, a decent studio by LA's standards, as well as a private restroom. It was a four-bed and two-bath place, and the other three tenants had to share the one bathroom – apart from Clark's. There was also an outside patio area, an overgrown yard in the back, and a washer and dryer for free use.

The two housemates Clark interacted with the most were constant bachelors with overnight jobs. One was in his fifties, a war veteran who only ate junk food and worked nightly constructed jobs. The other was a forest firefighter, so he was gone for weeks or even months at a time before resurfacing.

There was technically a third housemate, or room neighbor, but she was never home. The firefighter told Clark her room was just as much a royal pigsty as it was storage. She stayed at her boyfriend's place ninety-nine percent of the time. They were actually engaged, but were circumstantially live-in spouses trying to figure things out. Having never met her, Clark only trusted that to be mostly the truth.

The roaming snacker gathered that all the housemates knew each other before living at the house together. The construction vet broke it down to Clark one night as the older man finished some laundry before leaving for some karaoke drinking event.

They were family friends. Turned out the landlord was a notable contractor with his own business. Everyone converged on at least one of the landlord's projects. The missing woman was some sort of construction zoner who assessed policy risks for insurance purposes. The firefighter did construction before committing to fighting blazes. And the vet had worked for the landlord for years before learning of the room he had been renting. This was also before the fraternity showed up. He probably was not a huge fan of the ragers they no doubt hosted at home.

Six months into Clark's lease, everyone else decided to move out at the same time. A giant, wild coincidence. The firefighter was making amazing money doing what he did. He realized he could stay somewhere that was nicer and more on his terms, even if it was going to be for days or a couple of weeks at a time. And that likely gave him plenty of peace of mind, being the resident clean police.

The policy adjustor was finally getting wedding plans solidified with her fiancé. And they had just put money down on a home in Simi Valley.

The vet decided it was a good time to move to the Inland Empire – to be closer to his kids – who he could only see for a weekend a month in LA.

So it was going to be Clark, and only Clark for the time being. A king of his castle of a house. And that's when the angst to need to do something different, the need to cultivate a co-working space where professional magic could occur, first started to demand serious attention.

He emailed his landlord. It was the pitch. The business plan. The manner of sustaining money for a time to come; the way the bedrooms and living room could be slightly tweaked to accommodate desks and meeting stations, among thinking and break ones. And even the prospect of the trial of it all if it did not end up being the direction the landlord and boss man wanted to go in for the house.

Clark also texted him to check his email.

The solitary tenant stepped onto another street, the horizon of the end of MLK Boulevard just starting to come into view. He figured he had paid enough rent regularly – and on time – for his idea to at least be considered.

The thing was, he got a reply.

A third of his Doritos had been consumed at that point. Plenty of fuel left for the journey. It was a peculiar taste that helped him navigate his world through salt, pepper, vague but compelling cheese flavoring, and a slightly murky sky.

Clark was sure there was enough time to count the cost of such an ask. The yes or the no, and what either would mean for the next five years. Because success was usually counted in that interval.

He had enough of his snack to take an initial blow of misfortune in the hypothetical realm. If his landlord gave him the flat no, nothing would change. The house would be his for a few weeks before his new bedroom neighbors started to move in. He probably could not grab a couple of friends and simulate a co-working environment, in lieu of getting an actual one permitted – on account of the rooms getting a deep clean and scrub for the future tenants.

But the desire would be there.

He could attempt to build the co-working hub elsewhere. Earn a living doing the thing he finally felt comfortable admitting to himself, making a passionate effort where office management reigned supreme – in specificity.

Clark had also been working long enough, in general, to know it would not be the worst thing to not work where he slept. The thing he was submitting to his landlord was going to be just that. Would he have peace after everyone went home for the day? Would he be able to, at around 5 or so, drop everything and resume his tenant life? Without feeling the pressure to get just one more thing done to stay ahead of the demands for the next work day?

A woman smiling at her phone, at a nearby bus stop, was enough to pull Clark out of his head for a second. He thought it a flittering assurance that the cons were mostly emotional dangers of being too deep in. Something else his gut told him would be easier to handle, and to manage, than a bevy of problems that got his landlord involved in office affairs too often.

What about the positives of such a proposition? They did not come to Clark as quickly after he had done the necessary business of thinking of the out-of-home business – first – as a bad idea.

The thing that came initially, the cape around the man's neck that would drape over his mighty shoulders, was that he was solving a real problem. People needed to get work done. He could provide a healthy, ever-peaceful, and inspiring environment for individuals to work on what they saw fit. To further themselves and their visions of themselves.

If someone needed a room to write in, they had it. If another needed a room for an important phone call or interview, it would be provided. A one-stop shop for people and their businesses – more than a noisy coffee house that had all the outlets hogged before 8 am. Less than an office that required IDs and dress codes, and a need to always be vigilant for the slightest excuse to get fired, Clark's office would only require that the ambitious drive excels into graduating from the co-working space – one day.

Really, the guy was something of a coward. Even if he got all the go-aheads in the world to pursue the rented office space where he lived, and his landlord was also amenable to the additional pitch that in exchange for managing the space – his rent would not only be reduced a reasonable amount for the labor but he would also get paid a portion of the membership fees, Clark would still not be convinced any of it was a good idea.

There was strength in numbers. Working with the various clients daily would be the constant ministering Clark's soul required to keep up with it, to let it flourish beyond anyone's expectations.

He was sure, if he and his landlord built it, people and subscriptions would come. And on a revolving basis, making at least double what the old tenants provided in rent. The home was paid for anyway. But the boss landlord was probably looking for a profit after the funds for the property taxes had been secured.

Clark allowed himself to at least believe, even with the reply in his back pocket, that there was no way his proposal would garner an all-out no.

"Let me get one of those."

"A few more minutes. This is just the test dog. Grill is getting warmed up."

"I could be a lab rat, so long as you include some of those onions."

"By the time the onions are done, the other hotdogs will be looking better."

"I shall wait then."

"Looks like you've got an okay starter anyway."

The Los Angeles street hotdog. A staple. An institution. It felt like the right thing to do while Clark was walking and thinking, and munching. Though he would have been cheating at the fake game he set out for himself.

Consuming the hotdog would surely make the Doritos last all the way to his destination, but he was getting comfortable making up the rules as he went along. A metaphor for the challenges that lay ahead. The more substantial bite of food felt like it did not negate the earlier parameters in their scope. The dog was just a bigger thing to aim for.

"Everything?"

"Sure. Do you have water?"

"An extra dollar fifty."

"I'll take it."

"You want it now? Those chips must be building an aching thirst."

"You aren't wrong."

"A lot on your mind?"

"You can tell?" Clark asked. He was not trying to hide anything. But he did not think he was an open book either.

"Those Doritos look halfway eaten. When a baby is teething, give it something to chew on for its trouble."

"Think I'm at the corner of making a move or two. How is it for you, doing this day in and day out? The business and survival of it?"

"I struggle. But it gets me by. I got a lot of peace of mind that the people the world says are more successful than me would die for. I see it when I hand them their food."

The smell emanating from the grill gave Clark the fumes to develop just a little more confidence about where he was headed.

"Your turn. Grab a plate."

"That's it right there. Just trying to live with myself and do the things I want to."

The hotdog vendor cooked for a few minutes, letting a safe silence build between the two.

"Work is work, no matter how much you love what you're doing. But being true to yourself is hopefully the easiest job there is in this world. Four dollars."

Clark accepted the newly weighted plate of his lunch, then gave the man his earnings. And then some.

"Thanks for the food."

"Thanks for the company."

A wiser person would have been more content to eat the components of their meal with a little conservatism. You get to one thing and then complete the next thing. But not Clark. Forget the challenge.

He did need a few Doritos to cut through the richness of the street dog with everything on it. The hotdog was just what the walk ordered, but it needed a hard and crunchy chaser. He gave himself three chips with which to be the beef dog's companions.

The non-juggling act was a mostly successful endeavor, save for the drop of the ketchup-and-mustard mixture that crash-landed onto his left shoe's laces. The orange liquid, a poor attempt at tie-dye

Clark was not being all the way honest with himself. He did not want to be some passive office manager that only opened the facility up for clients, warned them of the last hour, and then closed things down until the next day. He desired, more than anything, to graciously host the vocationally determined. He wanted to feed their minds and mulling habits. Clark wanted to cook and clean, and be around to encourage the members.

With his ultimate aspiration, there was most definitely an ideal scenario.

He would wake up early and get ready for work – like most adult citizens aimed to do – between five and six am. It would be around seven for Clark.

Instant oatmeal would likely be the breakfast of choice for many days on end, with some coffee. A fried egg over buttered and jammed toast would be the extension on particularly hungry mornings.

Then he would start a little music while he wiped down all the workstations for the new day. The music would be turned up while it was just him, and then lowered to a tasteful elevator volume when the clients arrived.

Once he finished cleaning and prepping all the spaces, that would put him at around eight-thirty. The first of the reservation slots would start to come in by nine.

That was when all the refreshments, coming from a portion of the membership fees, would be put out. Continental things and other snacking items. He would finally go to Costco and not feel like such a weirdo for using the membership on only himself. The home office may even have justified bumping himself up to the business card.

He also could not forget to display the monthly drawing vase. The drawn winner would get a twenty-five-dollar coupon to a few local sponsors.

Then the time would come. That special time between the first of the members, and the rest of Clark's workday – the bulk of which would be done in the next twenty or so minutes.

It would be time to apply some easy math.

The host would grab at least four mid-sized plastic containers from the fridge, and a large – making five. He would then reach into an above cabinet for some liner. The eight-quart slow cooker would be sitting atop a counter all its own, hungry for a slow turning of brew and reduction.

It would be the secret to keep, the point of gaining a visiting subscription to the club. It would be the peace and solitude of Clark's home co-working. He would keep clients paying for months on end for the lunch hour. It would be the focal point on which the space would exist and would operate on a sustainable basis.

Between noon and one o'clock, lunch would be ready for all the clients – a complimentary component of their membership if they paid enough for it. But they would. Because by lunchtime, the aroma, the tease of whatever was on the menu would be screaming at them from a buildup of flavor.

There would be plenty to go around. And if there was some left over, the clients could zap the day-old food in the microwave from the work shelf in the refrigerator. Or they could have the special of next day's lunch.

Clark could not host, could not entertain, could not be *the* cafeteria lady to his clients – without something substantial to fuel their work output. The meal of the day would dictate the community volume.

There was the basic tier membership that only allowed for the rental of the various spaces of the facility. Then there was the second tier. All the spaces were available for use, and the members in the middle also had access to the pantry and drink fridge. There would surely be a smaller fridge near the kitchen just for beverages. Between Clark's personal food stock, and the Crockpot helpings, there would have to be more room elsewhere.

The mac daddy tier, the most expensive that awarded the best perks, gave its members full access to the workspace – most importantly, lunch.

Was Clark just some villain that got off on having master plans, or did he not have enough friends? He was not sure. But it did feel like easy math.

He had not mentioned his lunchtime dreams in the proposal to the landlord. He figured an outline of the tiers, and how they would support and maintain the space was adequate.

Down the line, once things got established, the landlord would be so impressed that things worked out. Entry into Dynamo Co-Fellows would be in such demand that a waitlist would have to be generated, because membership retention was so strong.

Clark had already been busy researching and cataloging three to four-hour recipes. A few seasonal meals. Concoctions for rainy days. And surely desserts, for a smaller slow cooker.

The landlord would wonder why. Why all the seemingly random success? What was that certain sticking agent?

Clark would be no snitch. He would just keep reinforcing the need for the upkeep of such a space in the age of social media, content creation, and good, old independent contracting. The landlord was one himself, after all.

That was the daily dream. Emotionally, it was also arithmetic. It felt like simple addition. And the equation was just getting set up to get knocked down by the landlord boss' approval.

Clark reached the corner of an elementary school. MLK Boulevard was home to several. Hope Elementary, an old mosque back in the day that turned into a private grammar school academy, was the last before MLK met its end at Central Avenue, which intersected it.

The destination was not far now.

Hotdog, downed. Just enough Doritos to go, Clark set out after the last of his walking excursion.

There was a majestic weight to the load Clark carried. It was the potential for many amazing things to happen, and the dream that doors could stay open beyond an excellent feeling. He felt like Santa Claus, lugging a hefty bag of gifts to the next home.

But there were a few things, past the cons, that could make Clark look down to check his foot placement on the ground – to make sure his shoes were tied.

He wanted to do his job. He would be happy to do it, but would it keep him without want? The money should be there, with the discounted rate for living at the property. But what about the difficult days, weeks, or months? He was already prepared to keep the space open at least two

Saturdays out of the month. But Sundays and major holidays were going to be days off, unwaveringly.

Clark was down to his last handful of chips. It was a good ride. He made it work. But keeping your own business afloat was an entirely different animal, undeniably.

He was not going to be in on this alone. A lot counted on the landlord giving the okay. The whole operation, in fact. The thing Clark needed the most for this to move forward was the very thing he feared above all else. He could not get the okay and let his would-be angel investor – as it were – down.

But there were squatters. How in the world would he deal with them?

Clark turned the corner from Central Avenue, which meant his sojourn had come to a close within mere feet. He had a single, uneven Dorito to spare. The steed helped him become okay with being a work in progress. But he was not going to let up on needing to get things done.

He crunched on his final chip and opened the door to the Hilltop Café.

"Nice to see you taking advantage of our setting," Clark said.

"I told you I had a taste for their tenders. Mostly the barbecue sauce. What did you have to show me?" Clark's friend, Maria, answered back.

"I've been thinking about trying a new thing out."

"Clark pulled out his phone. Opened the email app – to the audience of his friend.

"An email? You could have sent it to me. That's kinda the beauty of those."

"I need some active criticism."

"I am good at that," Maria reflected.

"I know and—"

Clark's face fell. He turned his phone to Maria in a quiet state of terror, so she could get a better look.

"What?"

"I didn't send the email."

"For what?"

"I'm going to do it. That office space I was telling you about."

"Who were you going to email?"

"My landlord. It was going to be a whole thing."

"So you needed me to go over the email?"

"I needed you to help me get through the reply. Keep a cool head about it."

"Send the email now. See if he says something before we leave."

"Can't."

"You didn't save the draft or something?"

Clark's face lined and folded further. His Doritos utility for his long walk started to develop a bad taste in his mouth. He could savor the crumbs and the seasoning he no longer wanted to.

"The email I thought was his response was actually an email for a rent increase."

"Ooof."

"Don't think he'll be too receptive to my big idea now."

"Lemme see the pitch."

Clark nearly tossed her his phone. With the knife driven into his ego, it was the best he could manage.

"Don't get any barbecue on my screen."

"Seems that would be the least of your heartache right now."

She dunked half a tender in her prized sauce. The liquid nearly flooded out of the cocktail bowl to accommodate her insertion.

"Maybe it's a good thing you didn't send it out yet. Already spotted two typos."

"I'm not writing a book. How does it read?"

* * *

Hi Jason,

Hope your day is going okay. I am reaching out to you today with some business. A proposal, in actuality, about what the future of the Washington property could be.

I'll start by sharing this link: https://www.wework.com/

As you have hopefully examined in the short video, co-working spaces are the future of the freelance workplace. These individual clients or small groups could most definitely find a reliable Starbucks, or someone's apartment to try to get some work done. But the type of workforce a co-working space attracts largely features the movers and the shakers of the world. They're starting businesses and companies all their own, and they need the atmosphere of an office for such crucial start-up operations.

Office spaces for rent aren't new. But the old model comes with more than a fair share of fees. And the overhead requirements are too corporate to cultivate any real long-term relationships with the clients.

A co-working facility is that place where you feel energized to go get work done because you truly have the space, the peace, and the comradery to do so. These workplaces boast an amazing retention percentage because the subscription member system and the comprehensive programming provide solid ground for reinforcing strong workplace values.

That brings us to the next matter – how does this model for renting out your home continue to make you money?

As mentioned a second ago, co-working spaces have more than leaned into the subscription-based structure that runs so much of our marketplaces already.

What maximizes earning potential is tiering the service. This would be three levels for working at 5629 Washington Boulevard that would range from basic to full access of the facilities of the elaborate home office.

Further, a revolving schedule of members will not only increase your monthly income for the property but should also triple it, assuming we can sustain a monthly rotation of at least 18 members.

This is where I would come in. I am also requesting, as the sole remaining tenant after May, that I be kept on as an office manager for the business and home operations. A service like this needs the right groundskeeper, and I would be committed to growing the business – from advertising to upkeep, to programming. And everything in between.

I'm not just asking because I already live at the house. My qualifications include running college dorm halls for two years, as a Resident Assistant, during my undergrad tenure at Channel Islands. I was also the runner-up candidate in the selection process for the Residence Life Council position at said CSU institution, for the entire dorm building. Needless to say, looking after people is an occupational interest of mine.

Another benefit to you: the start-up costs and initial investment won't be much. Each room – besides mine – will be made into an office space: desks, lights, and chairs. We would need some odds and ends for the kitchen. The communal spaces will require a little tweaking, but the frame for the work setting already exists. We have Internet. Just need to invest in a strong router setup to ensure broader signal connectivity.

Should this interest you enough to explore, I already have the legal paperwork handy to send over. You, the landowner, will be protected. The workplace would be free from certain liabilities. But as a grassroots operation, this will officially just be a handful of people coming over daily to get work done.

I would be more than happy to look into the earning potential for this proposed workspace more closely, especially from a monthly and yearly cost/revenue standpoint.

In addition, the nature of my tenancy would also have to be reevaluated, since I would be working for you and would require some compensation. Or a reduced rental rate for staying at and maintaining the property.

Hope we can make something happen, and thanks for being a gracious landlord, in any case. It is your care of and dedication to this house that has inspired such an ask.

Should you require it, I can easily send over a resume with references.

Feel free to call me as well.

Best,

Clark

DON'T DO STUPORS

THE FIRST PHASE OF THE war was getting to the Christmas dinner table, way across town, through scores of Los Angeles zip codes. But they made it.

Damon, and his sister, Amber, were part of the last group to arrive at the family function. There was always traffic coming from the south side of Downtown.

The eleven-year-old boy could not help but think that if his big, big sister, Flow, did not have to go twenty minutes out of the way to take him, their little sister, and his mom to dinner at Aunty Sheryl's place, then he would have had a premier seat at the table.

Flow was nearly fourteen years Damon's senior. She was out of the house. Had her own life to live. But no family yet, apart from what she grew up with.

He was not going to stay there, the dinner table. The adults sat at what was otherwise known as the grown table. But before everyone settled in their seats for the onslaught of scraping sounds, of chewing and sucking noises – the next phase of the war – Damon could usually sneak a seat and get his portions of food the way he wanted. As long as he was neat about taking the food from the baking dishes and serving plates so as not to trigger any of his older cousins or observant uncles into making comments that embarrassed his mother. In that case, his parent would provide him his plate with lackluster portions. Either way, then it was off to the kids and cousins table in the den.

Damon and his household rolled with Flow because his mother never drove on the freeway. Ever. It was absolute death to attempt such a trip anywhere. What if she got in an accident? The freeway crashes always looked like hell. Or what if she got lost? Then where would she end up?

She always made the lost excuse sound worse than a crippling car wreck. Although everyone else used the freeway just fine. Every year. Every day. Without so much as a cough in the direction of metal-twisting carnage.

Before they left for dinner that year, Damon's mom told him that was how Aunty Sheryl got her house. She was taking herself and her trays of food to another place for Christmas dinner, a bit before Damon was born. And she got into a terrible accident. Sheryl was okay, but the car was totaled. "And so was the food," Damon's mom chuckled. Chicken, soup, rice, and beans smeared all over the highway road.

The accident was far from Aunty Sheryl's fault, and she used the insurance money to put a deposit on the home where she currently resided.

After hearing that story, a certain anxiety crept into Damon's intentions. What scared him the most was not getting to the dinner. He looked forward to the family affair every year. Thanksgiving and Christmas were his Super Bowls. Strangely, it was the traffic that heightened the excitement, the anticipation of getting to Sheryl's house. Everyone else on the roads was headed to their meals, too. The quest gave Damon a strong sense of purpose, like being at the airport. And he did not even have to fly.

Contrary to all of Damon's mounted fears about not getting enough combinations of food on his plate – or the unfathomable – missing the start of dinner, he was usually able to eat all his little beating heart desired. But the conflated nerves about the euphoria of the first few bites of holiday dinner, and the thought of missing a portion of the meal, always managed to get just a little bigger every year.

The children's den was the other phase of the war. The two oldest cousins, around Damon's and Amber's ages, were usually commanding the conversations.

It amazed Damon how different each year of reunion would be. One year, everything would be jovial. They would eat. And have some real fun catching up. Then there would be some movie to enjoy or some new board game to gather around, and he and Amber would never want to leave.

In other years, the two commanding cousins of the den would not talk much. One would be deep in a book, no thing or no one as interesting as the words on the pages. The other was content to stay in her room throughout the evening.

Damon would later learn they had sleepovers fairly often since they did not live far from each other on the outskirts of LA County. The quiet holidays often meant they got into some quarrel during a recent overnight stay. The nature of which Damon could not get to the bottom of. Either his mom knew and did not tell, or she did not want him to instigate anything between Adelle and Draiya on his own. Thankfully, if the bad blood was still flowing for Thanksgiving, it was usually gravy by Christmas.

That year, it was going to be fine either way. Damon's mom let him have the Mature-rated ninja hack-and-slash video game he wanted. Turned out it was the hardest thing he ever played, but it was fantastic. Returning to his quest to confront the excommunicated spellcaster holed up in the mountains was going to feel better than starting the game for the first time.

No matter the holiday, or the year, getting on with his cousins was always a slow-moving engine before it started to really get pumping with liveliness and glee. Damon did not know why it had to be like that. He and his cousins were not all that different in age and interest. The spectrum of the den was seven to around thirteen years of age. Draiya was thirteen, and Adelle was turning thirteen in a few weeks.

He saw friends every day, and they were cool with each other. Even on the first day of school, after a summer of not speaking to one another, they always reconvened like they were in class the day before.

Damon and his cousins were all standoffish in the moments leading up to dinner, every holiday. They would not make an effort to say hello to Damon or his sister, and when Damon tried to initiate anything close to a decent conversation, he could not get the same enthusiasm back. He almost always was made to feel silly for trying to be so friendly and less nonchalant like Draiya or Adelle. Eventually, Damon would ask his mom how much longer they had to stay. She would say they would not be there much longer, knowing she was just trying to appease his boredom without actually intending to leave in the next half hour. Some eating and talking, and then back to the house? It was not how they or their family got along.

That was usually the cue for things to pick up. The night would shift, magically, to a warm evening of quality time with extended loved ones. Not a long night with related strangers.

Everyone would get some dinner and would relax. Opening mouths, for food, would just tend to stay open for one reason or another. Damon would hope his mom forgot all about his complaint. Which she typically seemed to do.

They were his family, his cousins. But they were the biggest people of mystery to the child. He saw them at church, but he really only got to hang out with his relatives a few times a year. The occasional family picnic, Thanksgiving, and Christmas.

Damon was never quite comfortable visiting because he was never at Aunty Sheryl's and Adelle's place too often. He was old enough to know there was a way you carried yourself when you were at another person's house. But he hated how much he had to be careful with people he was supposed to know better than anyone else. And his mom and big sister did not help much since they only broke down the proper way to be a guest when he was in a code-red violation of conducting himself as a good visitor. It could never be strictly informational for some political reason.

But the dinner would take everyone's edge off. It seemed Damon was not the only one who looked forward to the festive nourishment. Everyone just knew that all the pressures of living amongst people would be diminished for a time. Like a reverse gas tank.

Damon was all about the food, but the thing he would not tell any-one for a long time was that he just wanted to hang out with his cousins. It was the best word anyone had for relatives born of your aunts and uncles, but they were something else to him. He wanted them to be good friends.

"Dang, Damon! You'll be in a food coma, you eat any more of that."

Draiya made the comment that put the focus on Damon for a sec-ond. Something one of the oldest said usually did. He acted like it was nothing, but he enjoyed it.

"What grade are you in?"

"What video game is that?"

"Honors reading? Lemme see how fast you read this."

He answered with the same kind of deference his cousins had for the more benign questions he thought he asked them. Damon was not all that sure what a food coma was in the first place.

He thought his slightly older cousins did not have any cares in the world, that they always had some sort of sleepover or day-long playdate by the time the dinners concluded and everyone left. He wanted to be in on the perpetual fun since he assumed it would invariably feel like the family gathering would never conclude itself.

Settlers of Catan emerged. Damon nor Amber ever played, but by the time they learned, Damon did not care about his hot new console game that was waiting for him at his uneventful home. He hoped his mom would never come into the den the way she always eventually did when it was time to go home at the end of the evening.

He did come out momentarily for some 7-UP cake, a la mode. Not much could stop him from smelling that fresh, buttery aroma calling his name from the dining table. While he fixed his dessert plate, he heard Flow say she was leaving soon. He shot to the kids room, hoping they would not come looking for him and his little sister until the very last moment.

At least until they finished their second game of Catan when they truly understood how to play.

When the game ended and Damon came out of the den, brandishing his second-place bragging rights – with his jacket in his hands and his shoes on his feet, most of his extended family was gone.

They were nowhere in sight. And he heard the rest heading out the door. He did not see his mother or Flow.

"Aunty, where's my mom?"

Damon's mother left earlier.

What?

Without him? Or Amber?

She had to go to work for an unexpected night shift. Flow was supposed to take her siblings home, but she forgot, or she thought they caught the same ride with their mother back to LA. They did not leave together.

Damon and Amber were stuck. Until tomorrow morning.

The romanticized feelings of his aunt's place, those that made Damon pretty sure Sheryl's home rivaled the enchantment of ten combined arcades, faded quickly after having been abandoned.

The grand dinner table was cleaned up. The dining room got too dark once the overhead light fixture flicked off.

Damon and his sister had to share a bed. And a flimsy linen cover that Amber hogged all night.

The two did not brush their teeth. They slept in the clothes they wore to dinner. The free cable Damon enjoyed watching at his aunt's place lost its special holiday glow.

"Hey. Can I get a cup of water?"

"Help yourself. It's all in the kitchen."

"Oh, thanks."

Damon could not sleep. He rolled out of bed and sought to be some-place different. He was kind of heavy-eyed, but not enough to forget where he was.

He found himself in the hallway and caught Adelle emerging from the restroom, from what he assumed was a midnight tinkle.

"So your mom couldn't take you home?"

"Flow was supposed to."

"Yeah. Aunty Patrice doesn't like to drive on the freeway, huh?"

"No," Damon whispered, hating that it was too late to feel embar-rassed about anything. But there he was, not wanting to talk about how he and his sister – being forgotten – could have easily been avoided had his mother driven a little dangerously.

"What are you doing tomorrow?" He asked his cousin.

"I don't know. Probably getting vacation homework done a little. Then…I'm not sure."

"Is Draiya coming over?"

"She and Uncle Dom have to visit people tomorrow or something."

"Christmas is always over way too fast."

"I guess so," Adelle thought back. "But Christmas every day wouldn't be that special either. Jesus would just be another cute baby."

Damon could only nod and smile awkwardly in the darkness.

"Sweet dreams. Back to bed, I go."

In that lonely, cold hallway, Damon remembered what Draiya said about the food coma. Maybe that was it. Him being stuck between sources of light that made him feel strange in a new dimension – between the restroom light Adelle failed to turn off, and the fridge light that would help him quench his after-hours dry mouth.

He got so full of the holiday food he loved that he ended up in a peculiar place. It was once familiar, but he had no idea how he got to such a field of unidentifiable fuzziness. It felt like he was in a waking dream, and it gave him the carbonated sick sensation he experienced when Flow let him try beer once.

Maybe only one plate of yuletide food next year.

THE CREEPING THING

IT WAS SUPPOSED TO BE the perfect crime. No one should have gotten hurt. No egos should have been crushed. But nothing was actually wrong. As long as Terry stuck to his story. Or not have said anything. Probably better not to have said anything.

He always wanted to know what it was like to be a professional competitive eater. And seemed like the entrée and cake tasting for his wedding was going to be the perfect opportunity for some kind of externship assignment. It was going to be the variant of work-study that did not pay him anything. Just wages in more of what he was sick of, out of each passing day.

Food.

The thing that did Terry in from the start. But he could not shake the pining desire. So he had to be obedient, in tip-toe fashion.

Because of the wedding.

He and his beautiful wife-to-be had agreed that the best way to try the menu options was if they had more or less fasted for the day. It was not fasting, in so many letters. Breakfast was fine. They just largely agreed about not eating a big lunch.

In the way Terry usually royally screwed up, he not only violated the terms of their agreement, but he also did it in the worst way imaginable.

In the man's defense – and he did not believe it was a particularly strong one that would keep him out of the proverbial dog house, it was an organic explanation nonetheless. That should have counted for something semi-respectable.

The only other problem was that the defense still violated another promise the two came to terms with before the tasting pact.

But we are getting ahead of ourselves. We would have to start at the beginning. Terry thought it the most helpful to do so.

Not at the very beginning, but Terry could not believe he was marrying the love of his life. All the romance and development of his soulmate bond with Constance was well established in plenty of other stories.

The two even had a playful saga they would always orally improvise while on their dates. He would say his character was a mighty this. She would say her character was a force-busting that. Nothing serious. But their champions were often at odds before they worked together to take on the world around them.

What was required was a bit of contextualization. A certain kind of shading. A character letter that should have held up in court.

This occurred well into the engagement. But before the practicing groom committed the crime that was under present examination.

Terry enjoyed Chinese takeout. An understatement, admittedly. But to be certain, it was a favored fast food category, that in Los Angeles – not too far from the San Gabriel Valley – Terry had city blocks of. It was southern California. More than plenty of Chinese and pan-Asian places to choose from.

Terry's absolute favorite? He was a tad embarrassed to say.

It was not the hundreds of original hole-in-the-walls. Nor the dine-ins that sported a mom-and-pop atmosphere and were filled with generous amounts of house-made fast food staples. No, Terry enjoyed Panda Express more than the lot of them.

Pandas were reliable. They had quality food, and everything tasted as it should have.

If he were talking to more of the discerning customer about the cons of eating at a chain, he would admit that the food service and quality both had diminished some over the last two years, but the place still carried sides and entrees he would always opt for.

He ate so much Panda so often, Terry had the restaurant's app on his phone. He was on the news and promotions mailing list. He participated – actively – in their sweepstakes campaigns. The man did things for the restaurant most of the public never assumed existed for the quick service, American-Chinese food bar.

That was all until one day.

He and Constance had a conversation. It started when Terry mentioned, in passing, he was considering investing in the company that ran the Panda empire. It stopped his partner in her tracks. She looked at him and knew he was not kidding.

So they had a rather firm chat. About priorities and health, and supporting something that was not so corporate or opportunistic. The grand result: Panda only once a month instead of once a week. And once was his minimum. Through a desperate appeal, he got a pass to double up once every six months.

Back to the crime of the day. It had been committed in two areas. Terry was a hunger killer in two places on the day of the tasting.

He had been at work, just about up to the tasting, grinding away at his office responsibilities. The catering company was in Culver City and he worked in the La Brea corridor, closer to Inglewood. Per the terms of agreement B, he had not eaten much for lunch. He had not eaten anything.

Luckily, or unluckily, Terry managed to get off earlier that day. He was starving. He knew where all the Pandas were in a five-mile radius. One franchise sat three miles from where he worked. Another was at the Westfield mall, due northwest. The other, a very uncommon extension of a Ralphs grocery store.

He had to put something inside himself before the tasting so he would not be a grumpy Gus. But Gus needed to eat.

There were plenty of other options for getting a snack on the way to the wedding food interview. Something of a light starter to get the tastebuds dancing. There was a juice bar in the very plaza of the Ralphs-Panda. But he had to have his other love.

So he went.

Terry believed it was wisdom that told him at the last minute to look up an independent version of what he craved so. It would scratch the itch. Get him to the tasting. And he would be all eyes, ears, and tongue. So he did just that. The Hunan Grill Palace.

The problem with these non-chain establishments – really – their biggest strength was their lack of volume control.

Terry entered the restaurant with the best intentions. He did not want the full-service Styrofoam tray. The one with the large compartment at the bottom, and the two smaller spaces up top for the entrée portions. To Terry, it was symmetry at its best. But only some places offered more than one size option. Hunan Palace singularly offered the original to-go box. And a cup for soups.

Why would anyone complain? They hand the woman taking orders seven or eight bucks and she practically fills their plate from the dish to the ceiling.

Panda Express never did that. And most would see their stinginess at giving you a few extra pieces of orange chicken as a good reason not to set foot in the place.

Terry thoroughly failed at trying to get the poor woman to load up the soup cup with some vegetable fried rice and black pepper chicken, an attempt at a make-shift bowl accommodation. So he got the one-size-fits-all option.

This was Terry's big defense: Chinese takeout. But *not* Panda.

Constance could not get too mad at him, if she found out, that he at least tried to go off the well-established path a little.

Maybe she would have been okay with most of him breaching the contract. But there was a bigger problem.

Terry ate all of it. The rice. The chow mein. There was curry chicken that looked too good to pass up. And the broccoli beef had just been put out.

He loved it all. The man did not think about Panda once. Hunan Grill Palace floored his favorite with a couple of jabs and a shocking haymaker, and that was a hard thing to do.

But there were consequences.

Terry was wholly full. He did not need to eat the fortune cookie but he was on a roll. And there was still more curry sauce left to dip things into. He also did not need the Mountain Dew to wash the food down, but old habits died hard. There was never a Panda lunch or dinner he did not have with the fizzy, green beverage. But the carbonation was biting his mid-section early. He was not only stuffed but was also fit to bursting. He only came up for air after he had finished eating everything.

It was difficult for Terry to do things when he was full of food. Constance hated shopping with him at the grocery store if they ate dinner beforehand because his will to discern store items would always succumb to his lethargy.

There were ten minutes to go before he had to be at the caterer's. Terry prayed the adage about there always being room for dessert was a universal law. Though he was pretty sure it was a slogan for the Jello brand in the 80s. And their wedding was surely not going to feature something so lowbrow. Constance would melt from her heartache.

* * *

"DON'T YOU HATE GUM?"

Constance was waiting for her fiancé in front of the catering building. He was not late, but he was close enough to the deadline before they had to go in.

There was no time to check in with each other. To remind themselves to stick to the game plan, not to take the up-sales on the menu choices.

"Thought it a decent idea to clear the palette for the tasting."

"You weren't supposed to eat something so close to this!"

"I didn't. Just wanted to reset the tastebuds from the whole day. Plus, I was just bored."

She knew this was a commitment for Terry. It should not have been any other way, as she thought good principles needed to dictate their planning.

He usually had to try things out for a while before being okay with them. Though it was not out of a need to control him. She made sure her heart knew that any time they were trying to hash out the details of the big day.

Constance was going to make it worth his while.

* * *

"YOU WERE VERY AGREEABLE BACK there."

"I like to think we were just on the same page about the spread. Most of it seemed to be full of no-brainers," Terry responded. Rather promptly.

"Guess I can't disagree with that. The butterscotch crème chocolate cake is going to knock our guests upside their heads."

"Wish we had a spit bucket though. Who knew all that sampling would turn into a meal, right?"

"Aw, you can still eat, can't you?"

"Sure, babe. What did you have in mind?"

"Well, I know you were trying really hard to be on your best behavior for today. And it's not lost on me that you've given a good effort for the other agreement. So let's be naughty."

Terry's eyes widened with shock, but Constance saw something else in her fiancé's face she could not quite give a word to. It was probably a surprise to know she was treating him to his favorite. She was sure he knew exactly how they were going to indulge for dinner.

"Panda is up the street. How about it?"

"Yeah! Your treat, right?"

"Of course. And we still need a place to discuss the rest of the courses. Glad Miss Ann is giving us a week to evaluate everything else."

"I'll meet you over there. See you in ten."

"I'm going to get there ahead of you. Should I just get your usu—"

"No!"

"Okay..." Constance trailed off, certain then that Terry was in a strange place. So strange, she could not see where he stood.

"I'm in a different kind of mood today – a good one – so lemme think about it on the way over."

"Uh, you go it. Weirdo. See you in a sec."

* * *

THAT WAS TOO CLOSE TO call for Terry's sanity. He could not believe the predicament he got himself into. The food he had held so dear, the fast food he would have chosen over Constance in a variety of situations, was going to be the mistress that killed him.

He simply could not eat anymore.

Naturally, he was thinking of outs.

Work called. They needed a last-minute thing from him.

He was in an accident without his car being harmed.

Traffic was a mother.

Terry could not do it. There he was, trying to dodge a caring, loving thing his other half was happy to do – to put a smile on the infidel's face.

He deserved food poisoning. And then for his stomach to literally explode for eating so much earlier.

Terry was serious about the spit bucket. He thought that was a thing at tastings, but television – once again – had warped his expectations for real-life happenings.

That was no longer an issue. Terry was feeling it. The guilt and conviction of double-crossing his almost-spouse. She was going to have the last laugh. He was going to pay for a litany of things in the next twenty minutes.

But there was a softness to the realization that he could not mess around anymore. A grace from which there was a new kind of clarity. Immense fullness was just going to be his time served. And like slowly digesting food, it was going to stick with him for a long time.

He vowed to tell Constance one day, out of a broad spousal obligation to stay fair and true. Or tell the kids.

With his wife, of at least five years, it would be something to talk about while they waited for another thing to happen. While some food was cooking. While folding laundry on a lazy Sunday afternoon. Or it would be the kind of story they could chuckle about while out on a dinner date.

Constance would feel betrayed at first, but his silent prison would win her over. And she would giggle at the sitcom of it all once Terry pointed it out to her.

With their kids, the excess of food would precede a parental lesson. He would soften the blow of needing to get serious by demonstrating the importance of something within the story. They could only ever understand after hearing the conclusion: you don't trample over the ones you love with your impatience.

In more critical ways than one or two, he had done something he was not proud of. Lying. Betrayal. A covenant, no matter how practical and non-spiritual, had been broken. There was a slippery slope with the act, no doubt. It could lead to bigger, more dangerous decisions of disobedience. Sure. It had that potential – though Terry's resolve would never let him admit such a developed truth.

Ultimately, he did not wish to hurt the one he loved. No matter how small and innocent the act – for a moment of time – he did not take the woman's words, heart, and relationship seriously enough. That scared him more than anything else. But that was going to end. That day. In the parking lot of Panda Express.

He was going to respect his fiancée and stay true to his wife, even if she was not fully formed in the room.

* * *

"I KNOW WHAT'S WRONG."

"You do?" Terry asked as he greeted Constance upon entering the ordering line.

"The cake. You don't like the choice we made."

"That's not it, babe."

"No, it's fine. I'm not so sure it was the right choice either. But we can—"

"Con, the cake is fine. I just had some – indigestion was all. But I'm fine now."

"Now that you're at Panda, huh?"

"It's a solution more than you know."

"Did you figure out what you wanted?"

She really had no clue. She trusted him implicitly. It was another reason to take everything they had built and use it as blocks for the rest of their union. For the rest of their lives. This was only the beginning.

"I did. I might surprise you."

"Well, order away. You're up."

"Welcome! What can I get for you?" the associate asked.

"Baby?"

"Yeah?"

Terry was at a loss for words when the food came into view. On sight, his stomach warned him that blown chunks were ahead.

"You okay, Tare?"

"Fine. I'm good."

He turned toward the associate."

"Let me get a bowl today."

"Wow. That is surprising. You're going to eat an appropriate portion for once. Make that two, please?"

DATE #140 - EIGHT MONTHS BEFORE THE WEDDING

"THERE THEY WERE. WITHOUT KNOWING they were there."

"In the beginning, paths stretched through time, through space of land, where flowers and water and moss met, and they were merry under the sun."

"It would activate a certain buzzing from the insects. The creeping things always thought the sun was setting. It was too good, too heavenly not to be perceived as nectar. Their enchantment would sparkle travelers to believe that to be true. To never want to go past the hour of activation, but to keep resetting and walking to where the cool air was felt the most – where the air was most visible."

"One such traveler was on her way through the wilderness. She was not certain she had conquered where darkness and doubt were the densest. Though she was forced to know the place as a kind of womb from which she could emerge changed and transformed into knowing where she came from. It empowered her to press forward without knowing she was there with another. But she was determined to make her way through."

"Miles ahead, sat a placidity that rivaled the nearby river's. Knives adorned a torso. Other tricks of combat decorated a satchel. A worthy sword had the privilege of occupying a lap."

"He was fortified. Ready, in the clearing where most could be seen, but also in the warm sun that was hottest in the middle of the day. He sat, protected before the thing that compelled him to sit."

"A magnificent wall of stone was behind him. It was not as long, as it was imposing in the background. He could have gone around it. Others could have also found a way. But the mission had become one through which he had to apply himself."

"But there was no going through for the moment. He had tried. Brute strength and bloody knuckles. Dexterity and frustration. So the moment had turned into time to dwell on his efforts."

"Perhaps he needed help. It was fairly apparent. But all the serenity of the vast and easy ground he occupied could not make up for the fact that he was stubborn. And as someone who had a hard head, he was a patient one."

"He sat there, resting and waiting for someone who could lend a helping hand. Who could demonstrate the way not over or around, but through."

"He needed the credit. He was not sure what he would have done once he got what he was looking for, but he was sure the triumph had to be a solitary one."

"For her, the light came in the way of sustenance. The darkness of the wilderness was an unwanted swaddle, covering up what it did not wish to come out. But she managed to keep it at the corners of her sight with the foraging of berries and plants."

"Towards the edge of the leafy gloom, a trail of nectar started to form. It managed to turn on when the day fell outside. She filled herself with the seemingly endless supply of it, and the trail sustained her steps out of the towering vegetation."

"There was so much clarity upon emerging, though she knew not where she was. But where the nectar ended, she saved some liquid for going in the direction it pointed her to, and she continued to walk – noticing a structure in the distance."

"It was almost dream-like. Realizing he was no longer alone. That day, it seemed as if rain was going to get the best of the sunscape. Noncompliant, the light was making an effort to remain among the graying clouds."

"He believed he was aware of it before she was. She was approaching from afar, content to stay to the side of the road for anyone who cared to be faster than her. She carried a pouch she used to scoop up the fluid that kept her face aglow."

"She saw him when she was closer. Her eyesight, though it was not terrible, was not the best. He appeared to be some guard. To what turned out to be a brilliant stone wall."

"No discernable doorway. No indication it was the barrier to some-thing more desirable. But she got the impression there was something to encounter through its matter."

"He continued to sit, even as she was within striking distance. He had observed something that might not have solved his problem, but it would have helped. He was hungry. She had food. He needed her food."

"She stepped forward, unsure if she had to consort with someone so statuesque in front of the standing slab. She was determined to make peace, for she needed to make her way through."

"There was a sword lying within a measure too short for precision. He deftly grabbed it anyway, indicating he only wanted what she was eating."

"With so violent an ask, she could not honor the request. And she was sure the nectar was the key to the way through the stone."

"Once he saw she was not going to give up her goods, he made to press her further with more intimidation. But she just set her feet onward."

"He had to do it, had to engage her with his reliable arm of triumph, but she parried and avoided in a way he could not best."

"Their scuffle made its way to the surface of the wall. He grew winded, for he was fighting and was hungry. And she had the energy to exhaust."

"In a critical error of telepathing his fatigued sword technique, he fell against the stone. It was hard, but the cool resting place provided momentary respite from his attempted onslaught of taking."

"She saw he was powerless to do much else. Preemptively, she applied a hand to his chest. She made up her face – to exude more effort – and pushed through, his body and her hand breaking to the other side of the wall."

"The act made her lose her footing. They were both on top of the fresh rubble in a heap."

"There they were. Without knowing where they were. They broke through to something that looked familiar. There was more prairie land, and another patch of forest some hundred yards away."

"He was rejuvenated. Awake. The wall structure no longer possessed its imposing power, but it still held on to its beauty, being mostly intact."

"A new trail of nectar was visible a few steps away. She pointed. He obeyed."

"After filling his face, she helped him up. They started for the forest together."

THE LONG TAKEOUT

"I AM PRETTY SURE THIS is against corporate policy."

It was going to work.

They decided food was going to be their thing. However arbitrary a conclusion it was to reach after deciding to go to a focaccia-themed food festival on a whim, they were going to carve out their little corner of fame – one post at a time.

Gulliver and Sasha were family. Technically, ex-step-siblings. They were under the same roof for eight years before the divorce.

One would say the other was their brother or sister faster than someone could say heartbeat, but that label did not accurately capture their special relationship. Although, casually, it was the most approximate way to categorize what they were. Their bond had survived so much – lawyers and petty non-invitations to big family events. And funerals. There was nothing that could make them any closer than blood relatives.

Straightforwardly, they did not need any labels. The two hardly acknowledged them. Though in their mutual singleness, they were siblings when it came to filling in emergency contact information.

Gulliver and Sasha were the closest two peas in a pod ever since they knew the other existed. They did just about everything together, including working and living out their lives.

They were well aware of how tropey their connection was. Everyone thought they were a couple since a coincidental family resemblance meant they had to be romantically involved. But ironically, not brother and sister. Eww.

Neither was the gay best friend nor the beard to the other, which they started to encounter as accusations recently.

There was one implication of a particular stereotype threat, about a man and a woman not being able to successfully be best friends, without there being any element of sexual tension. Or some vague fulfillment of a porn fantasy. Notwithstanding, being practically sister and brother, romantic suitors tended not to understand their deep link to each other. More accurately, they did not approve of Sasha being so close to Gulliver, or the other way around.

So they stuck together, pouring copious amounts of relationship energy into their collaborative efforts.

No one had to look any further than their childhood to see it had been that way since they were kids. Lemonade stands, bike ramps, trading card collections – it was always a convoluted team operation to incorporate.

The two usually shared an equal amount of insistence on one scheme over the other. Sasha would be more enthusiastic about the clothing line that could not get enough angel investors.

Gulliver was all about the personal fitness service that promised two trainers for the price of one in a busy marketplace. Twice the motivation for the same market rate.

All were failures.

"It won't matter if we put the food back better than the restaurant had it," Sasha replied.

Social media changed their game at doing something successfully. There were more eyes. More tools to create a visible buzz. Better opportunities to crop around a single thing to tell people about, even when the two were inexperienced at whatever they attempted to get Insta-famous for.

The modern phone was going to be the great equalizer. No one cared what they did. It just had to be memorable and frequently occurring enough to create a following. They had to utilize all the tools to bring everyone's attention to their page. Just to say, "Look at us!"

And they would go from there. To what, they were far from sure. It was the oft-emerging gray area in most of their plans. Longevity. Spells and whiles.

If someone were to grill them on it, they would take turns explaining the merits of their current venture and how, in destined fashion, they would get picked up by some short-form TV production on YouTube. Or get some well-paying sponsors for their social accounts.

Gulliver and Sasha differed in a lot of the ways that close adult friends did, who came up in the world together. They had differing interests while still being joined at the hip. They worked dissimilar jobs and lived in different places – though not too far from each other. Never too far.

What they knew for certain was, some of their best ideas came to them as they hung out over food. They usually talked about whatever over a meal, but they felt good about most of their life decisions while sharing a platter, a basket, or family-styling something between them.

So it had to work because food always worked between them. It was the glue they never needed but always had in their possession.

The social media planet did not know what would hit them because the duo was not in the surest of vehicles themselves.

They just figured a three-pronged attack would give them an edge, serving their customers with more than enough content to have at between daily posts.

There was going to be the food. It was going to be the center and building block of Food-tertainment TV. A working name.

Most importantly, the network of content would post compelling food exhibits to the newsfeed, which would then entice followers and scrollers to the Next Up Food podcast.

It was going to be a radio show that explored old restaurant chain locations that were repurposed into new mom-and-pop food establishments. Gulliver's baby. On account of his major fascination with reclaimed Kentucky Fried Chicken bucket signs for new eateries.

Their last effort at garnering support in the form of likes currency was their joint review profile on Yelp. Who else was doing tandem restaurant reviews on the perennial review site? It turned out very little.

That was going to be the new thing. Sasha handled the Gram with posts. Gulliver headed the podcast effort, and the two attacked Yelp together.

Fame would most definitely be on the other side of their grinding.

Gulliver had a talk about it with Sasha, to be decisive about their group decision. He made her promise they would stick with it for a year and a half. No matter the volume of followers. From February, to around August of the following year, Food-tertainment was going to be the thing they would devote themselves to when they were not working, or hiking, or being best friends in some entertainment space. It was already complicated enough to establish, so they had to get a healthy system going before deciding to call it quits.

Sasha knew it would not come to that. At least not with their foolproof system of always turning over posts.

The other thing they had to do, because their entire operation hinged on paying more money than they had for food posts, was to find a sustainable way to showcase seductive dishes.

Sasha was already delivering food via a third-party app – a microcosm for the inspiration behind their hub of food media – she had no doubt.

Gulliver accompanied her on deliveries twice a week, or whenever he was bored, and they would capture the best delivery orders to submit to the world. Mostly to their growing network.

But how could food ever look appealing from a car?

The mode of photography usually had a good track record for designating subjects as pretty hot and tempting. Food could do it, too.

But Sasha did not drive a sexy car. The 2013 Honda Civic was reliable. Decent gas mileage still. But efficiency hardly sizzled.

The next best thing: a small surface area they could control and beautify – the exterior trunk – a container of sanitation wipes, a bit of small floral tablecloth, and the right backdrop of nature. Or something interesting going on in the background.

It was going to be their niche. They were going to be trailblazers in the produced, spontaneous shot. Some would say they were being poetic about food on the go. Or it would be a fun hashtag.

And more importantly, it justified the takeout containers in the pictures.

"We should have stopped here for our session. These hills are gorgeous."

"Yeah, but our GPS is out. We're so high up in these stupid hills, we can't even get the last of this dumb mile done."

"Relax," Sasha said, attempting to soothe. "We'll figure it out. They have to know their deliveries here will always be terrible."

"They didn't even tip us on the app."

"Which is why I really didn't mind stopping for this one."

"The Hollywood hills suck ass."

"You okay? Seems like something else is eating at you. More than usual."

Gulliver just sat and looked out the passenger window.

"Guess we'll talk about it later," Sasha mumbled.

"It's that one," Gulliver spoke up.

"You sure?"

"I've been counting the houses since we turned from Mulholland."

"Thank God you don't trust phones."

* * *

"KID STIFFED US A SECOND time," Gulliver huffed.

"Kid? His parents weren't home?"

"His first time ordering on his own. Twerp was mostly just thrilled it worked. Seems his parents didn't teach him about being courteous to the service industry."

"Don't tell me you lectured him on it. Is that why you took so long?" Sasha asked.

"The little guy happens to be a wiz with Legos. He showed me his playroom. Beautiful structures."

"I'm certain *that's* against delivery gig worker policy. But did it get you out of your funk?"

Gulliver did appear to be feeling better. He gave his best friend a smirk and got in the car.

"Good thing I don't technically work for them."

"Now help me with this post. It's gotta be at least 300 likes or bust before we get off this mountain."

"Can you put the phone away?" Gulliver asked.

"Putting the phone away – because I love you…"

"I'm ready to talk. I owe it to you."

"Why so serious? You actually okay?"

"Let me just say what I have to say."

"Oh, boy. Sure, bro. All eardrums."

"I want to quit Food-tertainment TV."

"Say what?"

"First, I hate how hard it is to say 'Food-tertainment.'"

"You knew we were going to do a dramatic rebrand eventually!"

"You love the name with your entire soul. It's not going anywhere. Just hear me out on the rest," Gulliver started.

"I thought we were in on this together. You said we couldn't bail on this one!"

"No," Gulliver responded. "I said you couldn't bail. And you shouldn't."

"What are you trying to get at? I can take it."

"This is your thing. I hope it succeeds. But the network can expand. And we can do different projects on our own."

"We do everything together," Sasha said feebly. It was hard to match her brother's sense of peace and firmness.

"We will. I just want to focus on the podcast a bit more. It can still be associated though. Maybe I can bring in someone else who is as interested in talking about these locations as I am."

"That's me."

"You'll always be the occasional guest. I'll pull out the red carpet for you every time."

* * *

THEY WERE LOOKING FOR THE place, the entrance, but they could not find it.

It was in some random hotel not far from the Hollywood Bowl.

They were at fault – a little – for arriving too early, trying to find something to do. With half an hour left, they decided to try to wait in whatever line was required before they could enter the event.

Weird thing was, Sasha and Gulliver found the hall when they tried to find it initially. But they were on the other side of the hotel. It was the press entrance. They had to go all the way around the building for the guest entrance. Of course, they could not walk through the hall where all the focaccia vendors were setting up their stations.

They were jealous of the media members instantly. What privilege. What prestige and influence. And their badges looked cool.

That was the very beginning. Despite the envy, their aim was pure. They did not quite know what they wanted the trip to turn into. The food and the people, in their various displays for one single piece of Italian bread, demonstrated to them how much you could care about one thing. Because one thing was not singular if there were shades to it.

Somewhere between the focaccia brownies and the Ligurian focaccia, featuring a fish cake finish – with the best miso soup they ever tasted – they understood what they could do; in some way, what had to be done from their throbbing sense of inspiration.

But the journey was also a tumultuous one from the start.

All the food was a rousing take on traditional and gourmet cuisine that looked to showcase the best of its ingredients. But the siblings were always going to be a ball and chain when it came to their commitment to each other.

Gulliver was terrible at staying put. His mind would wander, and he was always an awful victim at playing catch-up. Problem was, he was terrible at letting Sasha in on the intellectual big-bangs. So much so, they had to have a system when it came to grocery shopping. Neither, mostly Gulliver, could just walk off to find something. His rationale was, he could always find Sasha eventually. But it would waste too much time, before

Sasha would have to call and swear her brother to stay put so they could finish their store errand.

The food expo was no different. Gulliver just had to peek inside before trying to go around.

Afterward, when they were quite unsure of where to set their feet on the other side of the hotel, Sasha had to yell at Gulliver to quit walking so far ahead, so they could ask for directions from an employee.

The two peas loved each other, but certain matters always made them too anxious to try for things only so enthusiastically on their own – outside of their pod.

They were always going to be the champion in each other's corner though. Even if there were clear difficulties when it came to saying no. Focaccia was the perfect metaphor for the peer pressure between family members. The kind you felt silly resisting. But it could do more damage if you did not say no.

* * *

SASHA SAT AND STEWED. THIS was another area where the two friends, partners, and siblings delineated from one another.

Gulliver always wanted to deal with the hard stuff in the moment. Sasha needed time to come around.

"Fine. It won't be that bad to get our own stuff going every now and again."

"Thank you, sis. Sincerely."

"Can we get some falafel? I need to shove food in my face," Sasha asked and declared.

"You got time to talk a little more?"

Sasha looked at a sheepish Gulliver, preemptively wincing from whatever verbal onslaught was about to ensue.

"Don't tell me…you don't like falafel anymore?"

"Is there such a person? I just want to get separate plates. Your sides for the loaded platter give me gas."

Sasha nearly teared up. She opened her mouth – thought better of it – and just shoved her key in the ignition, starting the car.

"You are so footing the bill tonight."

FOR THE MUSIC OF GOING (EPILOGUE)

HIS HEART WAS FULL. AND he was full of snacks.

Someone from his college days remembered him. The associate chaplain.

He did not realize he told her so much. And so much revolved around what he was eating.

She caught him once. Munching on some chips while having a bit of quiet time in the chapel. In actuality, he just wanted to get away from everything. He remembered hearing during new student orientation that the interfaith building was pretty much open whenever, save for if it were occupied with an event. Otherwise, students, staff, general faculty – anyone could use the space to wind down.

He guessed he was being quiet as a church mouse that found some food because the associate found him digging in. It was not so peaceful.

But she let him finish his snack, as long as he did not make a habit of it. And as long as he indulged her with a chat before her next meeting.

They spoke about the space and the history that lived between the walls. The tip of the iceberg, as she put it, was the regular school programming – the convocations, weddings, and spiritual life events. The chapel also happened to be where the heroes of the school hid before they took on the world again.

The chaplain's words were engaging. They made him forget about his troubles. And in no time, she had to go. She encouraged him to listen to the air within the halls of the structure. He did just that.

He was not so sure if he heard much, but he felt good about heading to his afternoon class. The one that felt like finals week, every week.

He found himself back at the chapel several days later – trying to listen.

Sure enough, the associate came by again. She spotted the Kit-Kat in his hands, but he came meaning no offense. He brought the dark chocolate version for her.

So there they sat – and snacked in the middle of the pews, in the lower half of the sanctuary. Talking about the building they occupied.

There was another story that week about why special permission was needed to access the roof of the chapel, the very acts that led to the policy changes not long ago.

Once more, she had a gathering to attend. She told him to listen another time. And to try to engage more than just his ears.

Their weekly snack time rendezvous never ceased. The associate chaplain never stopped having a story to tell, and he never grew tired of listening. Until graduation.

Years had passed. He was getting ready to leave school and was high on the promise of taking over the world with his expensive education.

They were doing what they usually did every Wednesday afternoon for the last three and a half years. He brought some Andre Champagne with him then. The Blush bottle, from their signature collection – to mark the special occasion – since the regular kind was the golden standard for partying students on a budget.

It was likely going to be the last time they got to share in each other's company. And he still thought it fitting to celebrate the passing on of time and conversation.

He had gotten really good at listening. It was his main mode of growth, being away at school. And it turned out it was his weapon against occupying a strange land that left him unsettled. Being more ears than tongue led to A's. To yes answers for dates. It led to a greater understanding of his place of being, in the thick of many a human interaction. That included the phenomenon of golden solitude when no one else was around.

One of the last things the chaplain asked him, over peanut butter Oreos and bubbly, was what he thought the walls would say about him – to someone else – when he was long gone. Then he jokingly asked whether or not he had to be alive or dead for the building to speak of his existence.

She said an answer was not required at that moment. Just to let it pick at him a little in his times of quietness.

But he moved on. He forgot about the question. And life ensued.

Before the night of the unboxing, life was going millions of miles a minute. He was miles from being able to keep up. He wanted to but thought he was far too ill-equipped.

And then six walls showed up. Asked him to relax. Implored him to break some rules. They encouraged him to use his senses, which made his hearing stronger and his heart hopeful.

The associate chaplain was one of his best friends at school. He had never admitted something so sad. So syrupy. But she was a lifeline his mind had long drifted on from.

She remembered him. Remembered his moods. His various young adult and adult neuroses could not help but manifest in the chewing exercise of snacking. Crunching through processed and sweetened corn was training, and he was, once again, grateful for his workout partner.

The associate included everything they ate. Most of his favorites. Some of hers. The instructions, the Post-Its, were directions as well as memories. Building blocks – the letter described. He was sure to save the bags and wrappers, and got to crafting.

The result?

A square with a steeple. It made him laugh for a length. And surely she had something to say, as she always did, before she had to go off to the rest of her work day. She hoped the question stuck with him, and that the question – more than the answer – was a useful guide through the chaos and dirt of the world.

The back of the chaplain's letter added something else, not unlike the words she would speak, as he continued to look at the stained glass of the chapel. It was a way to go further.

"Listen for the outside. And go there."

He gazed at the formation on his bed. He stole a bag of cinnamon Teddy Grams from the corner of the snack chapel. Then he closed his eyes and listened for himself in the future. He was not sure if it was what the instructions asked of him. But he saw himself getting in his car. He envisioned driving off and not worrying about returning to food or clothes, or his own certainties about his failures.

ABOUT THE AUTHOR

 ELIJAH DOURESSEAU IS AN AUTHOR from Los Angeles, California. He currently lives in the San Fernando Valley with his wife, cat, and turtle. He is a writer exploring the depths and ends of food literature, along with all its fictional potential. His first two food-oriented titles: "Chalkboard Specials, For Those Who Need Shelter Inside" and "The Nasty Business of a Bodyguard" are currently available wherever books are sold.